SNOW IN ITALY by Kerry Weston

CHAPTER ONE

A bee buzzed against the stained glass window as the vicar droned on and a petal floated to the floor from the beautiful display of cream roses.

"and if anyone here knows of any reason why this man and this woman may not be joined in holy matrimony ..."

Ellie jumped and clasped her bouquet tightly in her hands, until her knuckles were white. She looked at the floor, clamped her lips together and held her breath . The moment passed without incident and Ellie breathed out and smiled at Maisie, the small flower girl who looked angelic with the sunlight turning her golden curls into a halo around her head. The village church was beautiful and still had all the old fashioned pews, with bunches of gypsophila tied to the end of each pew. Ellie had always loved this church and remembered going to the Christmas Eve children's service when she was a child. She used to love seeing the nativity, singing carols and having a christingle orange. Sadly she didn't have her usual sense of peace today, which wasn't surprising. The church was packed, it was full of brightly coloured dresses, hats and fascinators . She heard a baby start to cry and then the sound of footsteps as the child was taken outside. There was a full choir and church bells. Ellie mimed as 'All things bright and beautiful' was sung gustily by the youngsters in the choir. She was tone deaf and didn't want anyone to hear her. Mrs Brownridge's voice boomed out the loudest, she always thought she could have made it as a singer.

The ceremony finally finished and the bride walked down the aisle looking as beautiful as ever , although a little pale . She wore her long wavy brown hair loose with a few flowers scattered in the curls. A long veil of vintage lace flowed behind her and she lifted her dress to show dainty white shoes with pearls catching the light as she moved. Her new husband Ralph was busy nodding at his business acquaintances. Mrs Brownridge beamed at everyone, her wish had come true and her only child had married 'well'. Everyone trooped outside and were told where to wait by the rather bossy photographer. She had already had an altercation with the vicar, as she had insisted on moving a large sign for the church jumble sale. The wedding guests chattered amongst themselves until they were called for photos.

It was a lovely September day warm and sunny, with a few fluffy clouds scattered about. The church was built from golden Cotswold stone and was the perfect setting for the photos. Some American tourists were standing on the pavement taking photos. The church had appeared in several television programmes and often attracted tourists.The photographer could be heard shouting " no , no not in front of the gravestone. Over there ! " pushing the bride and groom and best man in the other direction. " Now the bridesmaids."

"Congratulations" Ellie hugged her best friend Sam and kissed her, she then pecked Ralph on the cheek, shuddering slightly as she moved away. Ralph gave her a tight smile from his thin lips. Really he wasn't that good looking, with his slightly receding black hair and pointy nose. None of that would have mattered, had Ellie felt he was good enough for her lovely, gentle best friend. At least she hadn't shouted her objections in the church. Now that would have made her popular with Mrs Brownridge.

An hour or so earlier Maisie's mum had dropped her small daughter off at Sam's house and carefully handed her over to Ellie, as if she were a parcel.
"She is so adorable " sighed Sam gently running her fingers through Maisie's curls "beautiful curls" " I haven't got curls" stomped Maisie indignantly "an' I want to wear shorts not that !" pointing at the delicate little dress, which had carefully been chosen by Sam.
"Please keep an eye her" entreated the mother rolling her eyes "she's a little monkey. Now you be a good girl Maisie. It's an important job being a bridesmaid, remember what I told you ? " Maisie nodded solemnly."It's probably best not to put her dress on until the last minute." and looking anxiously at her daughter she left.
"Don't worry we will make sure she behaves. Won't we Ellie?" demanded Mrs Brownridge glaring at Ellie.
Honestly, thought Ellie some people make such a fuss. Maisie had been golden, during the service. O.K. she had scattered the rose petals from her basket rather enthusiastically as she trotted down the aisle, but everyone had smiled at her, apart from Sam's mum who everyone knew was an old dragon.
Maisie had wanted to wash her hands in the front on the way out but Ellie managed to distract her. The photos outside the church seemed to go on forever and Ellie kept a firm grip on Maisie's hand.

"can I go and play now Ellie " asked Maisie, dimpling at Ellie

" Not yet sweetheart. You have been very good , but we just have to have a few more photos taken."

" It's a bit boring isn't it ?"

" Yes " replied Ellie " but Sam wants lots of lovely photos of us to keep for ever and ever." Maisie looked a bit doubtful at that and decided to pick her nose. At last they had finished and the photographer took the happy couple off for photos on their own.

"You can go to your mummy now sweetheart " said Ellie releasing her grip. Maisie headed off towards her mother.

Ellie was chatting to some old school friends when she heard a shriek from Mrs Brownridge, she looked around and there was Maisie standing by a gravestone. Her pretty peach dress was filthy and it was tinged with green.

"I thought you were looking after the child. Please try and be more helpful on Samantha's wedding day " she shouted to Ellie her double chin wobbling with indignation and the feathers on the awful hat she was wearing quivered.

"Here we go" sighed Ellie "Why does that woman always make me feel like a naughty schoolgirl ?

" Everyone was looking and smiling. Ellie rushed over to Maisie

"What have you been doing?" she hissed.

"Nuffink" replied Maisie, her big blue eyes looking innocently at Ellie "just rollin. I like rollin."

Maisie's mum rushed over.

"Oh dear here we go again"

"I am so sorry." said Ellie "I only took my eyes off her for a minute.I thought she was with you. "

"Oh don't worry" Maisie's mum reassured her "We have problems like this all the time. I made two bridesmaid dresses for her, the other is in the car. We put her to bed at night with a clean face and when she wakes up she is filthy. It's a mystery. You did well to keep her clean for so long."

Maisie was passed back to Ellie's care outside the reception. Ellie kept a firm grip on her until they were all seated for the meal and she was handed back to her parents.

Ellie helped Sam sit down, tucking her dress neatly around the chair and gave her a hug.

"I hope you will both be very happy " she said.

"Thank you." smiled Sam. "I know that you and Ralph have not always seen eye to eye, but I'm sure we can now all be friends. I am going to find you a lovely man, there are a few of Ralph's work colleagues and golf club friends here today."

Ellie smiled politely. Ralph was an accountant , so goodness knows what she would find to talk about to his colleagues. Maths had always been her least favourite subject and she hated golf. The reception was at the golf club at Mrs Brownridge's insistence. The room looked wonderful. Sam had been in charge of the decorations and the flowers as she had an artistic eye. She had managed to transform the rather dull room into an enchanted forest with large plants in tubs, huge displays of flowers and candles, in various shades of peaches and cream. Ellie helped herself to a large glass of wine and relaxed, chief bridesmaid duties were over and at least she didn't have to make a speech. Ellie always thought that that must spoil the meal for the one who had to come up with a witty entertaining speech. She knew she couldn't have done that in a million years.

Sam's father Frank stood up to make the speech. He looked as though he would burst with pride when he looked at his daughter. He made a good speech and as Sam looked up at her father Ellie realised how alike they were. They both had brown curly hair and merry brown eyes with a smattering of freckles across their noses. Sam was quite petite but her father was taller. He became quite emotional and had to fish a tissue out of his pocket when recalling an incident when Sam was small. Mrs Brownridge looked at him in disgust and the feathers on her large purple hat quivered. She had never forgiven him for finding marital bliss with someone else. Luckily Sam had inherited her dad's pleasant easy going nature. Sam's parents divorced when she was three, but Frank always made sure that he saw Sam every week, no matter how difficult Mrs Brownridge tried to make it. He often took Ellie on the days out and they always had a good time. Mrs Brownridge had tried to stop Frank attending the wedding and for once Sam had stood up to her mother and refused to get married unless her father was there to give her away, although she lost the battle regarding her father's new family.

"Oh Ellie didn't Dad make a lovely speech?" whispered Sam. Ellie nodded and blew a kiss to Frank who winked at her in return. Ralph's speech was rather pompous and boring and Ellie let her thoughts wonder. She looked out of the window and saw Maisie with her dress tucked into her knickers climbing a tree.

"Oh well" she shrugged "she is not my responsibility any more." and topped up her wine glass. She had not had much to eat during the day and so the wine was going to her head.

The meal was O.K. but not very warm . Mrs Brownridge had made a big thing out of the golf club's delicious food. The pudding made up for the previous courses, there was a delicious cheesecake with raspberry coulis.

"Oh no" squeaked Ellie when she put her napkin on the table. There was a big splurge of raspberry coulis on her lap. She made a quick exit to the ladies to clear it up and then stood under the hand dryer waving her dress about in an attempt to dry it. Her old school friend Emma came in and helped. You could still see a faint stain. Why oh why was she always so clumsy, she wasn't much better than Maisie.

"Don't worry " said Emma " It will be dark soon and no one will see it. I will walk in front of you when we leave."

"Thanks." smiled Ellie , she added some more lipstick and brushed her glossy black hair. At least she could take off the circlet of flowers now, it was getting on her nerves.

" Hi Ellie " said Mr Brownridge who had strolled over to the bar where Ellie was getting a drink "Doesn't my daughter look beautiful?"

"She certainly does Mr B" replied Ellie

"Please call me Frank, you are making me feel old. Do you think she will be happy with Ralph ? He seems a bit, well a bit straightlaced."

"I don't know" said Ellie "but I promise to keep an eye on her."

"Good girl" Frank gave her a hug and was then grabbed by a relative who hadn't seen him for ages. Ellie watched him fondly, by all accounts Mrs Brownridge had made his life a misery when they were married. Mrs B had refused to let his second wife Pat , Sam's younger half sister and his wife's son attend the wedding. Perhaps now that Sam was escaping her mother's clutches she could secretly visit her father's family. She often spoke about them and wondered what they were doing.

Ellie and her friends had a great time, they danced most of the evening. Ellie was introduced to some of Ralph's friends and had a laugh with them, they weren't as bad as she had feared.

"I hope your friend will be happy" slurred one of his work colleagues, putting his arm around Ellie "Ralph is very ambitious, he never comes to the pub with us after work." He wiggled his eyebrows at Ellie suggestively and asked if she would like to see his calculator.

"No thanks" laughed Ellie. She made her excuses after a while as she loved dancing and hadn't been clubbing so much since Sam had met Ralph. Ellie was a good dancer, she was very attractive with her long straight black hair and bright blue eyes. She had quite a big bust which she tried to disguise, although her friends told her she had a lovely figure. She tended to dance a bit wildly and the others had learnt to give her room. She managed to get her bracelet caught in Tom's hair and didn't notice for a several minutes. Poor Tom crashed around trying to follow Ellie, while the others rolled their eyes.

" Watch out Ellie's back " shouted Emma twirling around in the middle of their circle.

"This is great" shrieked Flo as she gyrated around Ellie, Matt,Tom and Emma. Ellie hadn't seen the old gang from school for ages and it was great to catch up. They retired to the bar for a breather.

"Hey " said Tom " did you hear about Rick? Aaron Green told me he had had an email from him to say that he was in the States and had been signed up for a record deal."

Ellie and the others exchanged glances.

"I hope Sam doesn't get to hear about this " muttered Emma " do you think she ever really got over him ? "

CHAPTER TWO

Ellie and Sam had not always been best friends. They had been in the same reception class at school and had played with each other a few times at playtime. Ellie was not the tidiest of children and quite a tomboy. One afternoon she threw a pencil sharpener to another child, but missed and somehow it hit Sam in the face and went in Sam's eye. Mrs Brownridge was furious and forbade Sam to have anything further to do with 'that scruffy child'. Ellie's mum made Sam apologise but Mrs Browning wouldn't change her mind.

"Never mind." shrugged Ellie's mum "you can't win them all. Come on lets go home and have a piece of chocolate cake."

Ellie was quite tearful

" I didn't mean to do it mummy. I like Sam " her mum gave her a hug and reminded her of the other new friends she had.

Sam was an obedient child and did her best to please her mother and so Sam and Ellie did not play together very much. Sam was a quiet dreamy child who was very good at art.

When Ellie and Sam were ten, Ellie was walking home from school with her long straight black hair escaping from a ponytail as usual, her school shirt untucked and her socks around her ankles. She noticed Sam sitting in the gutter crying.

"What's the matter" asked Ellie kneeling down beside her, her bright blue eyes shining with compassion.

"It, it , it's my blouse" stuttered Sam "I tripped over and cut my hand and now I've got blood on my blouse and mummy will go mad. She is always saying that I should look where I am going and I accidentally ripped another school shirt last week. "

"Don't worry come with me" smiled Ellie putting her arm around Sam "We'll go to my house . My mum will help and she doesn't shout."

Ellie's mum was lovely, she was a bit of a hippy, she had long wavy reddish grey hair. She was very keen on yoga and could often be found on her mat meditating, whilst her dad attended to his beloved garden and vegetable patch.

"Hello Sam, whatever is the matter " exclaimed Ellie's mum. She gave Sam an old T shirt of Ellie's to wear while she sponged the shirt and dried it. She also gave Sam a huge slice of coffee cake. Sam then rushed home, but from that day she and Ellie became firm friends . Sam was now older and more able to defy her mother. Ellie's home became a second home for her and she enjoyed escaping from her cold unwelcoming home to the happy home of Ellie and her brother Andrew. Fortunately Mrs Brownridge was often out at her bridge club, choir, playing golf or doing her half a day at the charity shop on the High street and as long as Sam did her homework and piano practice she was not too concerned. Ellie's mum fed her cake and allowed them to have picnics in the garden. They would also try out dance routines as they got older and became obsessed with music.

"I wish I had a brother or sister" Sam would sigh. Mr Brownridge had married a lovely lady called Pat but Sam was not allowed to see her. She already had a little boy when they met and then she and Mr Brownridge had a little girl. Sam really fretted about not seeing her baby half sister and one Sunday Mr Brownridge took Sam to meet his new wife, baby and stepson at a park. Sam had a marvellous time kissing her little sister and playing with the little boy, who was a year older than her. He had straight fair hair and so did her baby sister who was adorable with chubby cheeks and dimples. They allowed her to hold the baby. They were all lovely to Sam and played football while the baby had a nap. Mr Brownridge kept trying to tickle Sam and the little boy and they rolled around the grass giggling. Then they had a picnic with fizzy pop, which Sam was not allowed, crisps and huge slices of a gooey chocolate cake. Unfortunately she accidentally mentioned the football to her mother the following week and she was never able to see them again. Mrs Brownridge ranted around the house for a full week and stated that if he ever allowed her to see his new family he would never see Sam again. Sam sobbed in her room and couldn't understand what she had done wrong.

"I'm sorry sweetheart" said her father hugging her tightly the next time he saw her "One day you will be old enough to decide who you see yourself , but until then we must do what mummy says. I will make sure you see lots of photos of your little sister and maybe you could paint some pictures for her. "

Sam had nodded tearfully, but decided that when she was old enough she would go and see her dad whenever she wanted, she might even go and live with him and her little sister, that would show her mummy.

However difficult Mrs Brownridge tried to make it, Sam always saw her dad. She knew that he had threatened her mum with court, if she tried to stop him.

The girls were put in the same form at High School and were inseparable. As they got older they went out with boys and both liked long haired, rebellious boys, usually with clapped out cars, much to the disgust of Mrs Brownridge. When they were seventeen Sam fell madly in love with a boy called Rick who was the singer in a band he had formed called Miasma. He was very good looking with long blond wavy hair and green eyes with eyelashes that any girl would die for. Ellie went out with the drummer for a while but it came to nothing. Ellie was the livelier of the two and was always dancing and singing tunelessly. She went out with a variety of boys, but never got too involved . Sam and Rick went out for about eighteen months. Of course Mrs Brownridge disapproved. Miasma became more popular and were now booked for gigs around the country most weekends and so they didn't see each other quite so often as Mrs B refused to allow Sam to travel to the gigs. Sam attended art college near her home. She was gifted and had won a special art prize when she was in sixth form. Her mum had wanted her to become a teacher but Sam's father intervened and said that she could always become an art teacher if she wanted. Sam had loved art college and had met more like minded people. Ellie joined in with most of their social events and Rick too when he was about. They had some brilliant nights out together. Ellie had started work after sixth form. She had not really known what she wanted to do as she had no particular talents.

Mrs Brownridge had been plotting with her sister in Canada and when Sam finished her course for the summer Mrs Brownridge handed her an envelope.
"It's a present for all your hard work." she said.
Sam opened the envelope and found a return air ticket to Canada.
"Your Aunty May wants you to visit her for three months. You know she has no children and is fond of you."
"Thank you." said Sam faintly "but this means I won't be able to see Rick and Ellie."
"For goodness sake" exploded Mrs Brownridge "It's only for three months. They will still be here when you get back."
 Sam nodded dumbly and spent most of the next few days with Rick .
"Don't worry " he reassured her, we have loads of gigs booked for the next few weeks. We are finally making a name for ourselves . We are also in that battle of the bands competition next month and a lot of influential people will be there. We are practicing like mad. you never know when you

get back we might be famous." He plonked a kiss on her cheek and jumped on the sofa and played air guitar .

" Get off my sofa at once " bellowed Mrs B , making Rick jump and fall off the sofa catching one of Mrs B's precious Royal Doulton china ladies on the way. They all watched in horror as it flew through the air and crashed into the fireplace.

" I think it's just as well my daughter is going away for a while , don't you " and she propelled Rick out of the room while he was still apologising.

In the event Sam had quite a good time. Her aunt May was a much easier going person than her mother. She allowed Sam to have several long telephone calls with Rick, who told her how much he loved her and all the places they would go to when she returned. He was really busy with gigs anyway. Sam wanted to illustrate children's books and did quite a lot of work in the countryside surrounding her aunt's home and managed to build up quite a portfolio. When she returned home Sam discovered that Rick had just left for America . Miasma had been asked to support another band on their U.S. tour. He had left Sam a lovely letter, which he gave to Ellie to pass to her. He promised to write and phone. Sam received one letter and after two months the phone calls tailed off. Sam had been really upset and had moped around for weeks, she even thought of trying to get a flight and surprise him. Ellie persuaded her that it would be silly to use all her savings when Rick might be too busy to spend time with her .

Ellie had called round to Sam's house nearly every day and even Mrs Brownridge encouraged her to go out. Eventually Sam started enjoying life again. Ellie's mum had tried to get them to join her yoga group. They tried it once and at the end of the class they had to climb into their sleeping bags and meditate , both of them started laughing. It was the teacher's voice telling them to relax and float away that struck them as funny, but not the rest of the class by the look on their faces. Their sleeping bags were shaking and muffled giggles could be heard. Strangely they weren't encouraged to go again. An aerobic class was their next venture and although they didn't make it every week they still went most of the time. The class was on a Saturday and so they often called in to their favourite coffee shop for a latte and piece of cake afterwards.

"Oh it doesn't get any easier does it ? " puffed Sam, hovering over the cake counter and wiggling her shoulders.

Ellie shook her head

"ooh they have red velvet , I will have a piece of that and a caramel latte" she beamed at Deb behind the counter. Deb smiled and sent up silent thanks for the nearby sports centre which was a good earner for her business.

They used to visit local bars and clubs and had a wide circle of friends. They both had a few dates but nothing serious. They went on a holiday to Spain and met two men from Scotland and so that was doomed, but they had fun while it lasted.

Ellie had found a job after sixth form. At first she had tried working at the local vets. She loved animals and it didn't interfere with her social life. She had found it funny at first calling for 'Butch Jones' and 'Pickles Wood ' and she was quite efficient. However the third time the vet had prised her, sobbing, off a grieving pet owner , he said
" you know Ellie not everyone is cut out for this type of work."
" but Betty loved little Susie " sobbed Ellie
" I know " agreed the vet kindly " but they are comforting you and it should be the other way round."
Ellie nodded , she had been finding it upsetting. The week before a little girl had had to have her pet rabbit put down and she had cried all the way home.

She started to look for another job. Gemma a friend of hers told her about a vacancy at the local estate agents where she worked.
"I am not sure " frowned Ellie "Do you think I could do it ?"
" I don't see why not " retorted Gemma and she had been right. Ellie's bubbly personality cheered the staff and the clients and she had endless patience with the elderly clients. It helped that Gemma was dating the manager Mark and had put in a good word for her. Ellie found that she enjoyed going to work each day, trying to find the perfect house for their clients. Sometimes she showed people around the houses they were selling and she enjoyed looking at the houses and imagining how she would decorate them. She was part renting, part buying a small flat, but there was not much scope to do a lot to it. The staff all got on and they had some great laughs together. The estate agents was in the High Street of their lovely Cotswold village and so Ellie was never far from a tea room or clothes shop. The local honey coloured pub The Red Lion was an added attraction and did lovely pub lunches, although the landlord Ron was famously grumpy.

Sam had then been introduced to Ralph by Mrs Brownridge , as he was the son of one of her bridge friends. He was an accountant with great ambition. He had treated Sam like a princess and taken her for meals and to the theatre. Sam was unused to this treatment after dating Rick and others like him and had been flattered.

"I have tickets for Gilbert and Sullivan tonight Princess . The senior partner is singing. Please make sure that you wear that lovely outfit I bought you, won't you darling ?" He said.

"yes of course Ralph ." replied Sam

Ellie ground her teeth "What are you doing? You hate Gilbert and Sullivan and we decided that the outfit Ralph bought made you look about fifty." she hissed

"Oh I don't mind, it keeps Ralph happy and I wasn't doing anything else. He is really kind to me you know. I don't think Rick ever held car doors open for me or bought me gifts."

Ellie sighed . What was happening to her friend, she seemed to lose a little more sparkle every time they met. Ralph had never been particularly friendly to Ellie and told Sam that she behaved childishly when she was with Ellie. The two girls went out together on their own to avoid a strained atmosphere. The thing that worried Ellie most about Ralph was that he appeared to be totally lacking a sense of humour. She thought that Sam was glad of any kindness after growing up with her mother and she wasn't sure that Ralph was that kind.

Ellie had been thinking about this after her conversation with Ralph's workmates. Just before the happy couple went on their honeymoon Sam came over.

"Thank you so much for being the best bridesmaid ever. Let's do our dance before I go, I haven't had chance for much of a dance tonight. I will really miss you over the next two weeks, but a honeymoon in the Caribbean will be fantastic"

The girls had worked out a dance routine at school to 'A little respect ' by Erasure. They danced it now with a group of their friends joining in. Soon quite a few guests had joined them and other guests were watching and smiling. Ellie and Sam danced and sang and at the end they clutched each other and smiled for Ellie's mum who was taking photos . Ellie looked over and Ralph was standing watching with his arms folded and a look of disgust on his face, she didn't even try to look for Mrs Brownridge.

Ellie hugged Sam as she jumped in the car to leave on her honeymoon. Both girls had tears in their eyes. No one had quite dared to decorate Ralph's shiny car.

"Be happy and you know where I am if you ever need me,"

Sam nodded, they knew that things would never be quite the same again.

Ellie felt quite depressed when she went back to her little flat, she hoped that her friendship with Sam would survive the marriage and that Sam would be happy . She sighed and wondered if she would ever get married. If she did it would be to someone as unalike Ralph as was possible.

CHAPTER THREE

In the event the honeymoon had not been that successful. According to Sam the food had been too exotic for Ralph and he had spent a lot of time waving his phone around trying to get a wi fi signal so that he could check his work emails. Sam showed Ellie some photos but they were mostly of the beautiful scenery. There was one of both of them and Ralph was wearing shorts, socks, sandals , a long sleeved top and a strange hat. Apparently he has a bad reaction to the sun and mosquitos really like him. Sam looks tanned , but a little strained around the eyes.

" It was so beautiful Ellie " she sighed " you should have seen the sunsets and the people were so friendly. I want to paint some of these photos in oil. You would have loved the rum punch. Do you fancy another coffee ? "

" No I need to get back to work, but it was lovely to catch up. We must go out soon. Let me see the paintings when you have done them" and giving Sam a quick hug she went back to work , just in time for Mr Butterworth who was lurking outside the office to catch her and ask for an update on his sale. She could swear he spent hours waiting to jump on a member of staff. Probably because when they saw him coming the staff all picked up their phones pretending to be on long conversations.

" Same as yesterday and the day before Mr Butterworth , as I said we will let you know as soon as we have any interest and we can arrange a viewing." Ellie wasn't too hopeful as the outside of his house hadn't been touched for years. The tarmac had long since disintegrated and paint had peeled off the windows . Ellie had suggested a little spruce up of the outside, but her hints had fallen on deaf ears.The time he spent loitering outside the office, he could have redecorated the house.

Ellie sighed . It seemed unlikely that she would ever go skiing again. She went on a school trip just after she started high school and loved it. There was a later one that she would loved to have gone on, but it was in Canada and really expensive and so she never even showed her parents the letter. She and Sam had spoken about it but Sam wasn't as keen as Ellie and Mrs B hadn't allowed Sam to go on the school trips.Then there was the deposit for the house and so Ellie never had the funds, although she knew Gemma and Mark from work loved skiing. Now though she finally had some savings but no one to go with. She didn't want to play gooseberry to Gemma. Oh well maybe one day and in the meantime she would call in the travel agents after work and pick up a brochure.

Ellie arranged to meet Sam for lunch at The Red Lion the following month and Sam bounced in looking cheerful. "Ralph's away on a course next week. Do you fancy going out? Out out ." asked Sam

"Great " replied Ellie "let's go clubbing."

Ellie and Sam made sure they saw each other every week and spoke on the phone most days, but things were not quite the same between them. There was always 'the presence of Ralph' as Ellie thought of it. Sam was always nervously checking her watch and phone as Ralph was prone to checking up on her. He disapproved of her going clubbing and so they usually went for a quiet meal or a drink. Sam said that he even rang her when she was at the supermarket to see how long she would be and once he stood outside the toilet door saying that a particular shirt needed to be ironed in a hurry.

"I am thinking of getting a shed" joked Sam.

" Have you seen Barb and Ryan lately? " asked Ellie. They were two of Ellie's art school friends and had carried on meeting up regularly after they had finished art school.

" No " replied Sam " I never seem to have the time, we have to go to quite a few work dinners and Ralph likes to entertain some of his golfing friends or work colleagues at least once a month and you know what I am like at cooking. It takes me ages to prepare and clean the house and " she added " I am quite messy you know. Also shopping, washing and sorting out Ralph's dry cleaning seems to take forever and I have a deadline I am trying to meet for that series about Rosie rabbit. "

Ellie frowned , she was untidy, but Sam was fairly normal. She could be messy with her art equipment but they had made an office/ art studio out of the second bedroom so all her stuff was in there. Sam mostly worked from home and did the most beautiful illustrations for children's books. She always seem to be flustered these days. Ellie was worried about her.

"Just because you are at home doesn't mean that you are always at Ralph's beck and call you know. You need to get out and socialise with your own friends. We have some great laughs in the office and you don't get a chance to do that."

Sam shrugged " I know, I need to make more of an effort.I will start my effort by dancing all night."

Ellie picked up Sam in her old mini. It had a Union Jack design on the roof and Ellie was very fond of it, although it was prone to breaking down in inclement weather.

"Mum said that she will drop us off in town so that we can have a drink, as she is teaching Maypole dancing at the Town Hall and wants to get the room ready for the first session tomorrow. "
"I didn't know your Mum could do Maypole dancing." exclaimed Sam in surprise.
"She can't" retorted Ellie but they couldn't find anyone to teach it for the spring festival, so Mum bought a book and said she would have a go. She said it can't be that hard. I think it will be a disaster, you know she has no sense of rhythm. Still she said she will practice at home before she tries to teach the children. She only gets half an hour every two weeks as they are trying to slot it in with Brownies , but she has loads of time get it right. "
"Yes " smiled Sam "remember when she made us go to watch her in a yoga with music demonstration and she was facing the other way to the rest of the class through most of the demonstration."
Ellie grinned "Yes and we sneaked out when she was facing the other way."

At Ellie's mum and dad's Sam got a big hug off Ellie's mum.
"It's been ages since we saw you."
"Yes " replied Sam " I have missed popping in here and having a slice of your gorgeous coffee cake "
" Well if you help me with a quick maypole practise I will let you have a big slice to take home. I want to get it straight in my head before I teach the children. Did Ellie tell you ? "
Sam nodded doubtfully and settled on the lovely squishy sofa.

" Hello stranger" said Ellie's dad giving Sam a big hug.
"Now I know you girl's are going out ,but just try some of my elderberry wine. I think it's my best yet." He beamed as he poured two generous helpings.
The girls exchanged a look. Ellie's dad was always making home made wine and beer and most of it was disgusting. Ellie sniffed it dubiously and they gingerly took a sip.
"It's not too bad." muttered Sam.
Ellie nodded " a bit like port, but not quite so good "
They continued sipping their wine and munching on chocolate digestives. Ellie's dad topped up their glasses , thrilled that they actually liked his wine.
Ellie's mum took ages to get sorted . "I just want to make sure it works before I teach the children, I don't want them getting confused "
She tied long ribbons to the ceiling light and roped in Ellie's dad

" now you don't need to dance, just walk in the pattern I tell you."
The ribbons were already tangled. She made them all practice the easiest Maypole dance in her book,
"No not that way." She shrieked as Ellie's dad crashed into Ellie.
"Wait" she untangled the ribbons and checked her book .
" I didn't think it would be this difficult " she muttered. They all had another drink while she did this. Ellie suspected that her mum was looking at the wrong page, why was she having so much trouble ? The more they practiced the worse they got. Elllie, Sam and Ellie's dad collapsed on the sofa in a giggling heap.
"Oh I give up." said Ellie's mum in disgust. "The children will be easier to manage than you lot and there's more space in the Town hall. I'm going now, are you ready? " she peered at Ellie "How much of your dad's wine have you had? Your eyes look a bit bloodshot."
"I'm fine" shrugged Ellie.
The girls headed out of the house and Sam tried to climb into the back of Ellie's mum's car.
"Your mum keeps moving the car" she muttered as she tried to clamber in the back and then got her leg tangled up in the seatbelt. She slipped and fell sideways onto the car floor in a heap and then peered around in puzzlement.
"You can't take her out like this." said Ellie's mum.
"I know" sighed Ellie "I don't think she has been drinking lately. "
"No" piped up Sam from the back "Ralph shays it's not nice to see ladies who have had too mush to drink."
"This is all your father's fault." said Ellie's mum darkly "just wait 'till I get home tonight."

Ellie hauled Sam out of the car, although Sam kept protesting that she wanted to 'dansh'.
"I'm sorry love, I think this vintage is a bit strong." apologised Ellie's father. "I think you should both walk back to your flat. I don't think you should leave her in this state."
Sam insisted she was starving when they got to Ellie's and so Ellie ordered a couple of pizzas. By the time they arrived Sam had nodded off and she only managed one slice before she staggered off to bed.

Ellie sighed and put the pillow over her head. She could throttle Sam who was lying in the spare bed snoring loudly. She had heard Sam's mobile beeping several times, so she turned it off. So much for the big night out !

They managed to go clubbing the following evening and laughed about their 'quiet night in.'
"I told Ralph my battery had gone flat." said Sam looking guilty. "I think I need to apologise to your parents. It's all a bit hazy." Ellie snorted
"I think my dad needs to apologise to you. Goodness knows how strong that wine was."
They enjoyed the evening , although both of them had sore feet by the end of the night.
" Ouch I knew I shouldn't have worn those new shoes. " Sam was sitting on a stool rubbing her bare feet.
" Hello ladies would you like a drink ?"
Ellie looked up to see two men grinning at them.
" It's O.K. we already have drinks thanks " replied Ellie. The two men Greg and Stu were good company and were good dancers.Sam had introduced Ralph into the conversation, so that it was clear she was married. Ellie really liked Stu and when they were leaving he stopped and asked if she would like to meet him for a drink
" What are you smirking at ? " questioned Sam when she got into the taxi.

Ellie went out with Stu a few times until he told her that he had been promoted and was going to live in London. Neither of them were heartbroken to split up and they agreed to remain friends,
" You and Sam can come and stay with me for the weekend when I am settled , but don't bring that husband of hers, he sounds like a lot of fun." said Stu when they met for a last drink.

Over the next few weeks Ellie noticed her friend becoming quieter. She called for Sam one day and Sam was looking for her shoes.
"I'm sure I put them in the hall ready to go out." she muttered.
"Oh I put them in the cupboard." shouted Ralph.
"Honestly he is so tidy I think he has OCD." sighed Sam when they were in the car. " I caught him running his finger across the top of the fridge yesterday. He puts the dustbin out two days early. Why?"

"You are a modern woman with a full time job, Ralph should be sharing the housework with you. I haven't seen any of your oil paintings lately." said Ellie. Sam illustrated children's books for a job but she loved to paint in oils as a hobby. She had painted some beautiful landscapes and Ellie's parents had one hanging proudly in their lounge.

"Oh no" replied Sam "The oil paints give Ralph a headache so I haven't been doing any. I don't really have time at the moment anyway as I have had quite a few books to illustrate. Rosie rabbit's author recommended me to quite a few people."

Ellie thought her friend looked pale and stressed and it made her sad. Her friend was so kind and generous, but she had never been any good at sticking up for herself.

"You should tell Ralph that it's your home too." suggested Ellie.

Sam shrugged "Oh if I say anything he goes into a mood for days. Come on I am looking forward to this meal."

They went to Marios their favourite Italian restaurant . It was a rustic restaurant with checked tablecloths and candles. The staff knew them and were really friendly. There was a display with cakes, tarts and fresh fruit which they never managed to try as they couldn't resist the tiramisu.

"I wish I could cook food like this." sighed Sam running her finger around the bowl to get the last of the tiramisu. " I have found some recipes that I can manage now, but I don't really enjoy cooking."

"and me . I think I need to meet someone who can cook" agreed Ellie " mum is lovely but she is not really interested in cooking either. Last year she cooked the turkey with the plastic bag of giblets inside. It's a wonder we didn't all get food poisoning."

"she makes a good cake though" said Sam. Ellie had to agree, her mum's cakes weren't fancy, but they were delicious.

It was Sunday morning and Ellie was feeling a bit down. The weather was awful and her mum and dad were away for the weekend and so she had not had her usual invitation to Sunday lunch. The flat had been cleaned , the washing and ironing done and Ellie was bored. It would be so lovely to have someone to share Sundays with, to go for a walk, pop to the pub for lunch or even go to the cinema if the weather was bad like today. Ellie sighed, should she sew the seam on the blouse she wore for work, but she hated sewing. Cooking that's the answer!

"I am not going to eat junk food . I am going to become super healthy " decided Ellie . She made a nice salad for lunch and then threw all the vegetables she had into a big saucepan and made some delicious vegetable soup.

" mm this is really good" thought Ellie dunking her crusty bread into the soup. She decided to fill her flask with soup and take it to work. She had several house viewings the next day , so she would be able to have the soup between appointments, much better for her than her usual lunch.

"Morning" beamed Ellie at Mark the homeless man who was sitting in his usual place on the High Street. He was sitting on his sleeping bag looking hopeful.

" I am being healthy so no latte today "

Mark looked gutted as Ellie usually bought him one too, especially on Mondays when she often gave him a muffin as well. Ellie looked at his face and couldn't walk on.

" Oh go on then , it is Monday. Want a muffin? "

he nodded "Please and don't forget my three sugars." Ellie rolled her eyes at him and went in the coffee shop.

"At least I only had a latte, no cakes " she said to Gemma when she got into the office and was telling her about her healthy soup. Ellie told everyone about her soup, extolling the virtues of it and offering to photocopy the recipe .

It was 11.30 and Ellie was parked in the station car park having a well earned break. The second couple she had shown around this morning were very demanding and insisted upon looking in every cupboard and every nook and cranny. She had had to stop them trying to lift the carpet to look at the floor, which had nearly caused a side table to topple over. Ellie sighed and leaned back in her seat. she picked up her magazine and took the top off her flask, now for some delicious, healthy soup.

"Aaagh what was that ?" spluttered Gemma. She was absolutely covered in soup. It had exploded from the flask. It was dripping off her face, the ceiling, the windscreen and even the gear knob. She could hardly see the magazine for soup. She blinked and swore, wiping her sleeve across her face and clearing a circle on the windscreen with her sleeve. She didn't know where to start.There was no way she could do the next viewing she would have to go home and shower and get changed. Ellie rummaged in her soup covered handbag for her mobile. She rang the office.

" What have you done" exclaimed Gemma laughing. There was some muttering in the background then " Where are you? Mark said he will collect the keys off you and meet Mrs Samuels."

Ellie was busy using all the tissues and baby wipes she kept in the car to try and clean the steering wheel and gear stick, when she heard laughing.
"Stop it" she shrieked. Mark was busy taking photos on his phone and he was killing himself laughing.
"You have missed a bit" he pointed and Ellie felt the top of her head. She groaned , the car would never be the same. The smell was enough to put her off soup forever.

The next day Ellie went into the office and could hear sniggering behind desks. There were two huge posters by her desk with the title ' eat healthily and try Ellie's homemade soup' and there were two different photos of Ellie. In the one Ellie could clearly be seen with soup in her hair, on her forehead and there was even some on the end of her nose. The other showed Ellie's shoulder covered in soup and the dashboard and windscreen of the car covered in soup.
" I can't believe you lot. Call yourself friends ." shouted Ellie but she had to laugh . She had googled it and apparently soup could ferment in a flask. Back to muffins then.

Sam really laughed when Ellie told her about it and said she was going to ask Mark to send her the photos.
"The car still really stinks though and I have used so many cleaning products. I will have to have it valeted, that was one expensive soup. "
Sam smiled then sighed.
"What's the matter " asked Ellie
"Oh nothing , it's just that Ralph is having a hard time at work with one of his clients."
"Well he shouldn't be taking it out on you . If he does you come over to my flat. "

Ellie was telling her Gemma about Sam at work.
"You can't help her if she doesn't want to stand up for herself. " said Gemma "just be there for her if she decides to escape. Oh and it's your turn chasing today."
Ellie sighed, she mostly loved her job, but didn't love chasing the solicitors. It made her feel like the most unpopular person in the world. They were usually busy and some wouldn't speak to her at all and others sighed heavily and disappeared for ages before returning to say that something had come in on the matter and they would get to it when they could. She realised that they were busy

and receiving loads of phone calls each day from agents didn't help when they were trying to get their work done. She had built up quite a good rapport with the two local solicitors.

"At least you don't ring us on Fridays when most people are moving, or ring and find that we have received some questions from the other solicitors and then ring the clients asking them to chase us. Two agents have done that today , what with that and the system going down I haven't done any of the work I planned." muttered Jayne , who was Mr Patterson's secretary and usually quite cheerful, but sounded distracted today.

Ellie said that in that case she would leave her in peace.

"Thanks " replied Jayne " the trainee solicitor is supposed to be helping but he seems a bit overwhelmed and I am frightened that I will find him rocking in a cupboard one day ! "

" Eek " thought Gemma " note to self, don't apply for legal jobs."

She had received phone calls from two people today who complained that nothing was happening on their move and could she please do her job and chase the buyers. One suspected the buyer's solicitors were too slow and the other was concerned because their buyer's mortgage hadn't come through.

" yes of course, I will see what I can do Mrs Wilson." Ellie sighed as she put the phone down. Why did people not realise that you cannot make someone buy your house and these things take time. Most people were more willing to wait for a three piece suite to be made than wait a few more weeks for their sale and purchase go through. A house was the most expensive item that most people would ever buy. She sighed and carried on with the chasing.

"Wow look at the kitchen on this new listing ." said Gemma , shoving a glossy photo in front of Ellie. "bags I show the punters around this one."

"That's mine, mine, mine " interrupted Mark "hands off " and he retrieved the photo from Gemma. Mark was a great boss, he was always cheerful, his sandy hair was often standing on end and sticking out sideways. He was always running his fingers through his hair when he was going through his paperwork. He would then go into reception to see a client and forget to check in the mirror on the way out. Strangely he was a brilliant salesman, without seeming to put in any effort or hard sell. He was charming to the clients. The day before an elderly lady called in and asked if she could photocopy two pages. Mark refused any payment, but did arrange an appointment to view her house as he had shown her photos of ' a nice little bungalow' they had on their books and the lady agreed that the stairs were getting a bit much for her knees.

" A stairlift would have been cheaper ! " muttered Gemma out of the side of her mouth.
"We're all going to the pub tonight. Why don't you come with us?"
"OK" smiled Ellie "Who will be going?"
Ellie went to The Red Lion for drinks most Fridays. There was a good crowd of 'end of the week ' workers. Ellie had tried to persuade Sam to join them but she said that Ralph finished early on Fridays. They all had a laugh and wound down from their busy week.

"Like a virgin......." carolled Ellie tunelessly, the following week, while wrapping herself around the window display of properties for sale "oops sorry Mrs Daniels didn't see you there. Are you still looking for a nice maisonette ? .." said Ellie smoothing down her hair. Mrs Daniels glared at Ellie under her bushy eyebrows , while Gemma smirked behind her computer. Mrs Daniels had come in a few weeks ago and for some reason she had taken an immediate dislike to Ellie and always insisted on seeing one of the others. Luckily there weren't many like her.

Ellie felt lucky to work at the estate agents, it was local, her workmates were good fun and they often went out socially. Some of the things Ellie had done had to be hidden from Mark. He always reminded them that the customer was to come first, no matter how irritating they were. Although he backed up his members of staff if he could, even if he gave them a bollocking later
One sunny afternoon a young man walked in and demanded to see particulars for apartments. He never said 'please' or 'thank you' and would glance at each set of particulars and discard them without reading them . Ellie was becoming really hot and sweaty, as he had informed her that she must turn off her desk fan as he was allergic to dust mites. After looking through a mountain of sale particulars and then saying in a supercilious voice that he required something more up market than the properties they had to offer, he asked if they had 'such a thing as a toilet in this place' that he could use. Ellie was so annoyed that when he went to the toilet she grabbed the coke bottle that was sticking out of the top of his man bag and gave it a good shake. She felt very satisfied as she looked out of the window when he left and saw him open the bottle to take a swig. He was covered in a fountain of sticky pop and Ellie hid behind the window display choking with laughter.
Another couple were difficult throughout their sale and purchase. They called Ellie girl, clicked their fingers at her, telephoned or called into the office every day and insisted that she telephoned with a progress report every evening. It became a standing joke in the office.
"I'm not paid enough for this" she muttered hitting her head repeatedly against her desk.

"Oh bear with us not long now" encouraged Mark. "We will earn good commission on their sale and the house they are buying."

The day before the move they both rang Ellie at different times asking her to check with their solicitor that everything was ready for the next day.

" We won't agree to the sellers messing about. We want them out when our removals arrive."

" Well it does depend on the time your solicitors receive the money from your sale. They then have to send it on to your seller's solicitors and keys can't be released until then."

explained Ellie, grinding her teeth.

" I do not care about that girl, I want access to my new house. You have the keys right ?"

Ellie confirmed that she did.

Come completion day Ellie had been sweating as it looked as though the funds from the sale had been delayed, then she received a phone call from the solicitors acting in the sale of the house to Mr and Mrs Paininthebum .

"bet you are glad to get rid of this one " said the solicitor chirpily "you can release the keys." Ellie was pleased as Mrs Paininthebum had been sitting in reception for the last half hour, tapping her feet impatiently and demanding in a loud voice why 'the girl' couldn't just give her the keys now.

Ellie took the keys out of the cupboard and then looked pensively at the keys underneath. They looked very similar and belonged to an empty house that had been on the market for ages.

"mmm I wonder" said Ellie thoughtfully

 " Hi here are the keys, enjoy your new house" she smiled brightly and handed them over

"About time too our removal van is about to arrive" shouted MrsPaininthebum. " I can't understand why you have been so slow. I won't be recommending you to my friends !"

" I am so gutted and I appreciate the thanks for all my help " Ellie muttered waving her off.

The next working day being a Monday there was hell to pay. Mark explained that the Paininthebums had had to have the locks changed. Mrs Paininthebum hadn't gone straight to the new house, she had called at a furniture shop with the keys to look at new sofas. Her husband had insisted that the removal men were idiots who couldn't use a set of keys and by the time they had persuaded him that he had the wrong keys the agents had closed. "I hope this was a genuine mistake" said Mark glaring at Ellie after he had taken the call. Ellie looked at him with a hurt expression on her face. "After all I had done for them " she said sadly. Mark didn't usually get angry and so Ellie decided to grit her teeth and behave from now on.

There had been a few close shaves when Ellie thought she had pushed Mark too far, but she was good at her job. On one occasion she had persuaded a lovely old couple not to sell their house with a beautiful garden which they loved, for a flat. "A gardener would cost much less than the service charge on the flat." she informed them brightly. Mark had been annoyed, but was mollified when the couple's son came to thank them two weeks later and instructed them to sell his large house and adjoining plot of land. Ellie would always go the extra mile for the pleasant clients, particularly the elderly and young couples. She managed to sort out a mortgage for one young couple who despaired of ever buying their own home and they bought her a huge bunch of flowers to say thank you. Ellie found that it was often those with the least money who were the most grateful.

Gemma noticed that Ellie had been quieter lately, she had overheard her ringing Sam to see if she was free for a meal. Ellie put down the phone sighing " Ralph has got her caddying for him this weekend , as someone isn't available and Sam hates golf. We usually manage to get together when he is playing." She looked really down in the dumps.
Gemma swung around her chin length bob flicking across her face..
"Please ring Mr Lerone, he thinks he spoke to you yesterday, his first name is Toby."
"It doesn't ring a bell " frowned Ellie picking up the phone "Hi is that Toby Lerone," The penny dropped and Ellie saw Gemma grinning at her "Ha ha very funny, that was the switchboard for Cadbury's " she threw her rubber at Gemma.
The whole office joined in that week, she had 'Ann Tique, G String and Anette Curtains' amongst others. "Tell her to pull herself together " laughed Ellie. It did cheer her up a little though and she promised to join them in the pub at the end of the week as long as they stopped.
" I surrender, now stop it before I accidentally swear at a client."

At the end of the week Ellie went for the drink after work with Gemma and the others, even though she was feeling tired and still felt a bit down. The chilled glass of rose cheered her up and after several she ended up being persuaded to go to a nightclub. Gemma knew Ellie rarely turned down a chance to dance. Ellie was dancing when a tall good looking man joined her. He was a good dancer and they had a laugh and went for a curry together afterwards. His name was Greg and he was good company, although he did talk about himself quite a lot. He offered her a lift home and stopped on the way. He kissed her and Ellie enjoyed it, she hadn't had a good snog for ages.

"come back to my flat," he whispered huskily "it's only around the corner."

"Not tonight , I've only just met you."

"Come on, what's the matter with you ? " replied Greg tetchily "I've bought you a curry."

"Oh you've bought me a curry, so you think I should sleep with you, do you? " stormed Ellie " I offered to pay my share. Have you ever heard of getting to know the mind before the body." She opened the car door, threw him a note and slammed the door. Her exit was spoiled when she caught her jacket on the car door handle and had to open the door again "Why can't I meet someone special?" she thought a tear trickling down her face as she stomped off down the road.

Sam rang Ellie in a panic

"I've got to entertain some of Ralph's work colleagues, they are all partners and he said it's quite an important dinner. He wants to impress them as it will help with his promotion."

Ellie snorted as cooking still wasn't one of Sam's talents.

"Ellie how do I defrost a leg of pork in half an hour. I forgot to take it out of the freezer this morning and I need to start cooking it. Ralph bought it from the butcher's especially last weekend "

"Dunno, perhaps you could put it in the shower" replied Ellie whose cooking skills were non existent.

"Do you think that would work" said Sam doubtfully.

"Well I'm no chef so I don't know. What about a hairdryer? Better google it "

Sam rang Ellie two days later.

"How did the meal go?"

"Don't ask" moaned Sam "Ralph has been furious. I tried different ways of defrosting and the meal looked O.K. even if it was an hour late. Ralph said the guests had a 'mysterious illness' the following day and he is barely speaking to me." Her voice shook and she sounded so down that Ellie was furious.

"Tell him he will have to take them to a restaurant next time. Do you want to come over for a coffee later? "

"I can't we are going to Ralph's parents." replied Sam miserably." His mum is a fabulous cook and she is always pressing complicated recipes on me to try. She keeps hinting that Ralph is looking thin and underfed. I will see you next week. I have told Ralph that I am not doing any more caddying. I hated it. " Sam sounded as if she was about to burst into tears.

Ellie popped out of the office at lunchtime and saw Sylvia, her mum's neighbour. She had lived next door to Ellie as long as Ellie could remember.

"Hi Sylvia been shopping ? "

Sylvia was carrying a large bag and looking slightly bemused.

"yes I appear to have bought this " and she showed Ellie a bright pink furry coat.

"Was Mrs B working in the charity shop today then ?" asked Ellie.

Sylvia nodded glumly and walked off.

Friday evening drinks after work and Ellie was waiting at the bar, tapping her fingers. She was gasping for a drink.

"think the barman's gone on holiday " said a deep voice next to her. Ellie looked around and saw a tall, very tall ,well built man wearing an expensive suit. Ron appeared and totally ignored Ellie and the man while he emptied the glasses from the dishwasher.

" It's O.K. he is punishing you for complaining " whispered Ellie. The man raised his eyebrows and made rude hand gestures at Ron whilst his back was turned. He insisted on buying Gemma's drink, " Otherwise you might die of thirst. Hi I am Joel I am here on business. Don't suppose you know anywhere good to eat around here, everywhere will be closing by the time I get home"

Ellie told him that Marios was very good and he retired to a table in the corner and worked on his laptop. When he finished he came over to chat to Ellie and persuaded her to join him for a meal.

" I hate eating alone and I know that you will be excellent company " he smiled." The meal will be on expenses."

He was very attractive, although not really Ellie's type, with his cropped hair and manicured nails. He smelt divine and was obviously not short of money. Ellie was hungry and decided she would never meet anyone if she didn't give people a chance. Joel turned out to be charming company and had some entertaining stories about some of the people he met through work.

Joel put down his knife and fork with a contented sigh" That was great you were right about this place. I would like to see more of you, I don't live too far away and it would be lovely to meet up." He said wiping his mouth on his napkin." now what do you recommend for dessert ?"

" That would be great" beamed Ellie sipping her wine " and I recommend the tiramisu"

" excuse me I must go to the ladies." she rang Gemma whilst she was in the ladies and gave her an update.

" He is really nice and I am going to see him again."

When she left the ladies she dropped her debit card as she was squeezing her mobile back into her overstuffed handbag. She bent down to pick it up and heard Joel on his mobile. She was hidden from view by a large plant.

" yes darling, I am still stuck in the meeting so I don't know what time I will be back. Give the children a kiss from me and tell them I will take them swimming tomorrow."

" The bastard " fumed Ellie. She quickly walked towards the exit , grabbing her coat from the coat rack on the way past." I hadn't even had my tiramisu !" She then noticed his smart overcoat and backtracked. She plucked a handful of lemon slices and olives from the bar and stuffed them in his pockets , shame there wasn't a trifle handy !

CHAPTER FOUR

The first Monday in January thought Ellie sadly and I didn't manage to meet anyone over Christmas and New Year. She had had a whale of a time at the firm's Christmas do, until she had fallen off a table while singing along to the music and Gemma had put her in a taxi, which was all a bit embarrassing. Other than that she had only been to a couple of pubs. maybe she should try a dating app. Back to work and it would be ages before another Bank holiday.

Ellie was gazing dreamily out of the window and in walked a smartly dressed man .
" Can I help " said Ellie brightly.
"I certainly hope so . I want to learn to fish and I do not want to learn in anyone else's lake so I require a five bedroomed house with a lake. "
Ellie blinked and Gemma smirked at her.
"Right well my name is Ellie and we will do our best to find you a house. Are you available for viewings today ? "
"Yes" he replied tersely " I do not go back to work until Thursday."

Six hours later Ellie returned to the office and slumped in the chair.
"How did it go ?" Mark queried.
"well he said the lake at the first house was more like a duckpond, so I went large after that, but there was always something wrong with the house. Honestly he is so rude and he keeps calling me Hetty. I corrected him the first couple of times but now I have given up."

It was the same story the following day, but Mark was keen for her to persevere as the client was looking at high end properties. On the third day Gemma said " Cheer up last day."
"It's ok I think I have something up my sleeve."
The client had mentioned that he would not require the house for three years as he had signed a contract to work in Dubai. He then wanted to retire and also fish presumably.

Ellie picked up the client from the station.

"Now then Hetty I hope you have something better for me today as you have not done very well so far."

Ellie gritted her teeth and smiled. She drove through one of her favourite Cotswold villages, which had three picturesque pubs, several upmarket restaurants and shops. He seemed quite taken with the village, particularly the lovely delicatessen and then she showed him the lake which was only two miles away. He decreed that it was the best lake he had seen and not overlooked as it was in twenty acres of land. Then he saw the old farmhouse with a saggy roof, broken windows and collapsed chimneys and started to turn a shade of puce.

"You would not be expected to live here," Ellie explained hurriedly. "There is planning permission in place for demolition of the farmhouse, with a five bedroomed new build in its place. The council have indicated that they are amenable subject to a few tweaks."

Ellie strolled into the office carrying her favourite latte , with a smirk on her face. "Well ?" enquired Mark

"you know the old Woodbridge farm that we have had on the books for two years ? Well I think I have sold it." grinned Ellie. Sure enough after showing the plans to an architect friend the customer was very excited and put in an offer near to the full asking price, which was promptly accepted. She received a bouquet of flowers a few days later 'thank you Hetty for all you help.'

Ellie was not a morning person. She always closed her eyes until she had been in the shower for ten minutes and then slowly got ready and had breakfast. She did not become her usual bubbly self and start chatting until about ten a.m. On Friday she hummed along to the radio, glad that it was Friday at last. She jumped out of her car and made her way to the office. She stopped and frowned. Why was she walking with a limp? She lifted one leg and then the other.

" Oh no I am wearing odd boots ! " One of her boots had a heel, the other was almost flat. At least they were the same colour, she had worn one navy boot and one black boot last year. Too late to go home and change now and she had no viewings today.

She limped into the office feeling quite cheerful. It was payday, also they had six completions going through, so that would be a few properties off their hands. . They had all received a good bonus and Ellie's was helped by the lake sale completing in record time, mostly because he had terrified the solicitor into working at breakneck speed before he left the country. Then Ellie realised that she didn't really have anything to look forward to, no summer holiday or weekend break.

"Right that's the third time you have sighed in the last five minutes." said Gemma "You are coming out to the pub with us after work tonight."

"OK' sighed Ellie " I may as well I've got nothing better to do."

"Thanks" said Gemma darkly.

"Sorry I seem to be getting into a rut and this horrible January weather doesn't help."

One of the completions had been delayed and Mr and Mrs Robinson were stuck in the removal van outside their new home. They were a lovely couple and had not caused them any trouble.

" My solicitor said he sent the money an hour ago and so the seller's solicitor should receive the money at any time" said Mrs Robinson, she sounded close to tears.

" Tell you what, you come here now. I have the keys and will hand them to you as soon as I get the go ahead. I can stop in the office a bit later."

" Thank you, thank you " beamed Mrs Robinson clutching her keys at 5.30 " we would have had a terrible weekend if you hadn't hung on."

At the Red Lion they were sitting chatting comfortably on the leather sofas and shouted to Ellie when she limped in.

" your noisy lot are over there " indicated Ron the landlord " tell 'em to keep the noise down. We are not in a night club you know."

Ron was famously grumpy so Ellie ignored him. The Red Lion was handy for the office and a lovely pub. It was quite popular with tourists, which was good for Ron as by the time they realised how unfriendly he was they had already ordered. One person had put on Trip Advisor that he was the Cotswold's answer to Basil Fawlty.

" Thanks for doing that " shouted Mark " Your first drink is on me."

Ellie was sipping her much needed double bacardi and coke, when Gemma's friends, Will and Kate bounced in looking excited. Kate worked at a travel agents and explained that a group of eight who had booked to go skiing late February on a work related team building holiday, had had to cancel.

"They have offered to transfer the holiday to me and a group of friends at a reduced cost." said Kate "Will and I went skiing at the beginning of January but my manager said I can have the week off. We have six places left, who's interested?"

She showed them the brochure and it did look lovely.

Gemma and Mark were keen to go and so were Max, Melissa and Carly who were all single friends of Gemma and Mark.

"What about you Ellie?" queried Melissa, a kind girl, who was very curvaceous with wonderful long strawberry blond hair.

"Oh no I will be needed at work." muttered Ellie. She was interested and would have loved to go, but she didn't see how three of them could have the same week off.

"That's true " said Mark

"Oh no" cried Gemma " Ellie really needs a break and she has always said that she wants to go skiing. Can't you think of something ? "

They all sipped their drinks and looked at Mark expectantly

"Well " said Mark "I've been thinking we could get Rita and Ted in for the week. I'm sure they won't mind" He went off to ring them on his mobile. Rita had retired about six months ago and Ted two years before that.

"Go on live a little" nudged Gemma. Mark came back grinning.

"They would both be happy to help, they seemed quite keen. It's a quiet time of year ."

"O.K." grinned Ellie "count me in but I can't ski. I went with the school when I was twelve and can't remember a thing. "

"Don't worry, I'm the same" reassured Carly " and Max and Mel are complete beginners."

"I'm going more for the apres ski " grinned Melissa" I don't think I will be very good at skiing."

" Will your limp be better by then do you think ? " queried Carly.

Ellie was so excited , she couldn't wait to go skiing. The days were carefully marked off the calendar and she started doing squats every day in the hope it would make her fitter.

"It's in Italy at a place called Barganaga in the Alps. The hotel is called Hotel Girasole and the reviews say that the food is really good." she told Sam who had volunteered to go ski clothes shopping with Ellie.

"I wish I was going" Sam sighed wistfully "I always wanted to learn to ski . Mum would never let me go with the school and I was always a bit nervous to be honest. Gemma and her friends are good fun, but Ralph said we need to save for a new bathroom. Let me know if you think I would be able to do it and maybe we can all go another time" Ellie looked at her friend anxiously, Sam looked paler and thinner and it didn't suit her. Sam was petite and slim and had no weight to lose. Ellie had carrier bags stuffed full of socks, gloves, ski trousers and a jacket. The man in the shop advised her to buy a ski helmet, as everyone wore one now.

"Come on " puffed Ellie " lets go to Marios I will treat you to lunch."
Sam brightened they both loved Marios and tiramisu. It had been a standing joke when Frank Brownridge took them to lunch on a day out that they had to check if tiramisu was on the menu before agreeing to eat there. Marios did a wonderful creamy tiramisu and Frank jokingly timed them as it disappeared off their plates at the speed of light. The girls marked tiramisus out of ten and Mario's was a nine and a half, they had never had a ten.
" no need to ask what you ladies want for dessert " smiled the waiter
"That's better" sighed Sam licking her spoon . " That red ski outfit really suits you"
"I'm a bit nervous" admitted Ellie "You know how clumsy I am I hope I don't make a fool of myself or break something."
"You will be fine." Sam reassured her "You have to become a really good skier and then teach me and you might meet the man of your dreams."
"It's a deal." grinned Ellie
"Have a lovely time." said Sam hugging her friend.
"I wish you were going' sighed Ellie "Gemma and Mark will be together and I only know the others from the pub."
"You will be fine. Text me a photo of your hunky instructor"
"No chance of him being hunky" replied Ellie glumly "I think that's an urban myth. The instructor I had on the school trip looked like an umpa lumpa and kept shouting ' No No No you are not at disco now' because I kept wiggling my shoulders. Anyway I will steer clear of all Italian men particularly instructors. There might be someone nice in my class though" she added hopefully.
"Is that your mobile ringing?"
Sam sighed " It's Ralph. He probably wants to know when I will be back.I will pretend I didn't hear it."
Ellie noticed that Sam was on edge after that and left soon afterwards.

Sam was quiet that evening and even Ralph noticed.
"I will book a table at that French restaurant I went to with the office. We can go on Monday night, they do a special deal on Mondays. We can talk about the new bathroom tiles"

Sam smiled and thanked him half heartedly. She knew he was trying to be kind but she had heard about the restaurant, it was really stuffy with waiters in penguin suits and minute portions. Sam and Ellie had always enjoyed going to lively, informal restaurants with plenty of atmosphere.

"Better have a good lunch then. " she muttered to herself.

"What's that ?" Ralph frowned

"Nothing. I just said I had better not have much lunch."

"Quite right" agreed Ralph "Don't want to be wasting my money eh! If you are doing the ironing now I will show you how to do my collars properly and my Mum always used to iron my socks and pants. I can't understand why you don't."

He frowned as Sam left the room, surely she hadn't meant to kick his golf trolley in the hall on her way out.

CHAPTER FIVE

It was dark and freezing cold when Ellie woke up, but she never minded getting up early for a holiday. She lugged her suitcase to the front of the estate agents . She had packed ski gear and jeans. It seemed strange not to pack any clothes for going out and as instructed she had left her handbag behind and put her money and passport in one of the numerous pockets of her ski jacket. It was pillar box red and looked brilliant with Ellie's long dark hair. Books were a great love of Ellie's, she and Sam were avid readers and always carried 'emergency books' with them. Ellie had packed four, although she hoped there would be too much going on for her to read them.

Max and Carly had already arrived and they stood stamping their feet and swinging their arms to keep warm. The others came soon after.
"morning everyone" squealed Gemma
"shush" said Mark "people are still sleeping.
A minibus took them to the airport and they all went to the bar for a pre holiday drink. Ellie loved airports, they always felt exciting and she loved poking around the shops.
" I might just have a coffee " said Mel. She was shouted down by the others, so they all had a drink and said 'cheers to a happy holiday' .
"Don't have too many pints." Gemma warned Mark "Or you will be getting up and down for the toilet on the flight."
"Take no notice" said Max passing Mark another pint.
The girls decided to sit together on the flight and as predicted Mark and Max kept getting up and down and squeezing past the cabin crew.

Ellie felt really excited when they landed in Italy to blue skies and sunshine. Foreign airport buildings always smelt different and if you closed your eyes, you just knew you were on holiday. They found their coach and settled onboard. The first part of the journey was along a motorway and then they left the towns behind and could see the pretty countryside, with rows of olive trees and vines which had not yet started to grow, The pretty villages they passed were full of houses with terracotta roofs , which looked cheerful , even on a winter's day. The houses became more spaced out . The coach climbed up steep winding roads and Ellie began to feel anxious as there was no sign of snow.

The coach had to stop when they were going through one village as there was a parked car on the other side of the road. The coach inched its way through, just missing the walls of the houses and shops , some people in the street stood and watched. Everyone gasped and pulled their legs in. "Don't worry " said Craig, their cheerful rep. "The drivers go up and down these mountains every week in winter." The rep started to talk to them about ski passes and lessons and Ellie was relieved to hear that there was plenty of snow in the resort, as it had snowed three days ago. There were also snow cannons which could add to the snow. She nodded off and woke as the coach stopped at the first of the hotels. The light had started to fade , but Ellie could see snow all around and pretty Alpine village houses, shops and hotels, showing lots of twinkling lights. The rep had told them that Switzerland was on the other side of the mountain. It looked like a perfect Alpine village. There were children with rosy cheeks and colourful scarves pulling sledges, shops with pretty window displays and a small cafe displaying mouthwatering cakes and a sign advertising thirty flavours of hot chocolate. Who knew ?

The Hotel Girasole was small and friendly. It looked Swiss and had huge icicles along the side of the building, together with a pile of wood and on the way past the bar Ellie could see a cosy log fire. A plump woman greeted them smiling broadly.
"welcome to Barganago I am Maria an me an' my husband Enzo will look after you at 'otel Girasole an' my daughter Isabella she 'elp after school".
There was a tiny lift so they took it in turns sending up the bags. Ellie had a huge key, she would have to make sure that she always left it behind reception. The rooms were lovely and warm. Ellie was given a little room in the eaves, which looked out over the street. It was really toasty in the room and Ellie opened the window and looked across the road. There was another hotel opposite and then a spectacular backdrop of mountains covered in snow and lit by the setting sun. The air smelt different, it smelt of wood burning stoves and clean air. Ellie took a deep breath and smiled. She was going to love it here. She had decided to pay more for a single room, as she was not that close to the other single girls. Max had done the same being the only single man.They had been told to meet the rep in half an hour so that they could sort out their lift passes and boots ready for their lessons the next day.

Ellie walked into the hotel lounge and was handed a welcome drink by Craig the rep. It was really cosy with chairs arranged around the big log fire. There was another party of eight people, who looked as if they were in their fifties. They were very friendly and explained that they were a group of friends who had been going away skiing together for years. They had been to the resort two years ago and said it was really good for beginners which reassured Mel. They laughed a lot and obviously knew each other well. There were two other couples who had come together, they looked as if they were in their late twenties. They had been on their coach and had made a few know it all comments when the rep had been telling them whats what and hadn't smiled and said hello like the other passengers. They said that there was not much point in attending the meeting as they already had all the facts and were keen to sort out their lift passes so that they could make an early start. The gang christened them ' the smug marrieds". Other than that the other hotel guests were Italian.

"Oof" groaned Melissa "There's no way I'm ever going to get these boots on."
'Hang on I'll come and help" grinned Ellie "I'm just remembering what a pain it is to get these on." She pushed and Mel pulled and then they struggled with the fasteners and eventually Melissa's boots were on.
"Phew I don't fancy doing that every day" she said wiping her brow. Mel was a lovely friendly girl but had no self confidence. She didn't realise how pretty she was with her peachy skin and strawberry blond hair that fell straight down her back, almost to her waist. She decided that they fitted and they were given skis after the man had sized them with the boots. He showed them where they could leave their skis each day , instead of taking them back to the hotel, which was a relief to the less fit members of the group.
" The skis all look the same " remarked Mel " how will I remember which are mine ? "
The man advised them to take a photo of their skis to avoid confusion. They trudged back to the hotel together. It was dark now and the lights in the houses and hotels looked really inviting.
"I'm glad that I will be in Max's group." confided Mel "I have liked him for ages."
"Well" advised Ellie I suggest you fall over in front of him a few times so that he has to help you up."
The girls giggled as they put their boots in the basement room.

They went back to their rooms to get changed for dinner. The dining room was cosy with wooden beams and bright red tablecloths. There was a huge selection of wines ranged against one wall and a window looking out over the mountains. Isabella was only young but she smiled and read out the meal options in English. She said she was pleased to practice her English and she was top of her class in English and wanted to be a teacher when she grew up. Maria looked on proudly. They enjoyed a couple of bottles of delicious red wine. The meal was lovely, there was soup or pasta followed by slices of beef and vegetables. Ellie was disappointed that there was no tiramisu, but had a beautiful zabaglione. She had never tried one before and texted Sam to send her a photo of it. They took their wine glasses to the bar and sat in front of the log fire. It was wonderful sipping a drink and chatting and feeling the warmth of the fire. Enzo chatted to them and tended to the fire, he was the only person allowed to put fresh logs on the fire for safety reasons. He showed them an old wooden pair of skis hanging above the fireplace.

" This is what people wore many years ago and they had no ski lift " he explained.

"Wow imagine that "said Mark "It would take ages to walk up the mountain each time you wanted to ski and those skis look really hard."

They decided on an early night as they were all nodding off.

" yes it is good idea" smiled Enzo "you need to be up in morning for your lessons."

"Oh dear " muttered Mel to Ellie " I hope I can sleep. I am a bit worried. I'm not very sporty you know."

" you will be fine " Ellie slung her arm around Mel and they went upstairs. Mel and Carly were sharing. Carly told them both what they would need for the lesson.

Ellie opened her bedroom window. The air felt cold, she scraped a handful of snow off her windowsill and threw it at a car parked below. The lights of the village glowed brightly and in the distance she could see twinkly lights from other villages. She sighed happily and jumped into her lovely warm bed. The pillow and duvet were so soft. Unpacking hadn't taken long and she had her own ensuite bathroom. The next thing she knew it was morning and she was ravenous for breakfast. The smug marrieds were just leaving as they arrived for breakfast. Apparently they liked to get off early so they could be first on the slopes. They were all wearing backpacks and looked very professional. The gang all tucked into the buffet breakfast of bread, pastries, fruit and yoghurt. They also had wonderful hot chocolates and cappuccinos. Ellie noticed that Mel didn't eat much, she was looking worried.

The gang put on their boots amidst much grunting and groaning . It was only a short walk to the ski hire shop to collect the skis and the ski school meeting place was next to the shop, yet they all huffed and puffed, except Will and Kate who were obviously much healthier specimens. Ellie and Gemma pulled Mel along as she seemed to have a problem walking. She stopped for the third time and said she didn't think she could make it. Gemma bent down to look at her boots

" That's your problem " exclaimed Gemma " you have fastened up your boots tightly. It's better to leave them unfastened at the top until you are ready to put on your skis, or you can't bend your leg properly"

" The trouble is no one tells you these things and I know nothing." grunted Mel

" Think he is our instructor ? " grinned Ellie pointing to a tall instructor with longish jet black wavy hair. Her eyes had gone straight to him, he was lovely. Just then he turned and looked at them. "Wow he's nice, although I preferred that gorgeous one who is a snowboard instructor " replied Carly pointing down the hill " but I think that's our instructor and she pointed to a small wiry woman with dyed red hair who was coming towards them.

"Just as I thought " sighed Ellie "I told Sam this would hap....." but she stopped as the woman walked past them to a group lower down and the hunk walked over to them

"Hi I am Dario and I am your instructor" he smiled showing white teeth against his suntan and designer stubble.

"Thank you God." muttered Carly "What a wonderful accent he has."

Ellie didn't say anything she had been struck dumb. It wasn't often she saw someone she really fancied . She felt as though she had been hit by a thunderbolt. He was tall and wiry, with bright blue eyes and had a scar running down one side of his face. He looked as if he could be in a band.

"Oh no " she muttered " I can't fancy him

a. he's Italian

b. he's a ski instructor

c. Carly seemed to like him and any man Carly wanted she got

I bet he has a different girl every week." She decided that she would resist him and was so busy concentrating on this that he had to ask her three times for her name.

"Oh sorry it's er Ellie"

"Erelee " he frowned "I do not know this name."

Ellie blushed scarlet as she tried to explain. Dario gave her a lazy smile and shrugged.

"It does not matter beautiful lady, we will now see how you all ski."

"Ugh how predictable." said Carly rolling her eyes "still I'm going to try and get his attention, he's one of the best looking Italians I have seen so far, although I might book a private snowboard lesson."

The snowboard instructor Piero was extremely good looking with perfectly cut jet black hair, a deep tan, dazzling white teeth and bucketloads of charm. He was not Ellie's type and Ellie hoped he would take an interest in Carly.

Carly had a reputation as a flirt and it was a rare man who could resist her. She was small and slight with a short dyed white blond urchin cut which clung to her high cheekbones. She had big brown puppy dog eyes which she fluttered frequently at any hapless male in her vicinity. Ellie sighed, it was just as well she wasn't after Dario as she wouldn't have a chance with Carly around fluttering her eyelashes. Ellie slowly put on her skis. It felt strange after all these years and she felt a bit wobbly. Dario took them to the nursery slope first so that they could find their ski legs. Carly managed to fall over several times so that Dario had to come over and help her up, she also inveigled herself next to Dario on the chair lift when they progressed to a higher slope and chatted to him happily. Ellie was no good at flirting, she had once tried batting her eyelashes and smiling at a man. She then heard him say to his friend that he thought that poor girl had something in her eye. She was so busy watching Carly in action that she didn't concentrate as she got off the lift and she zoomed straight ahead and into the barrier. She was wrapped in bits of plastic tape and so embarrassed that she tried to get up too quickly and surged forward again knocking over two Italian men who were chatting to each other on the other side. Ellie was mortified. The men disentangled themselves good naturedly and helped her up. Ellie could see Dario coming towards her.

"Grazie, grazie " she smiled at the men "sorry, sorry." and she quickly skied towards the group.

"Are you ok Erelee?" questioned Dario

"Yes yes sorry" she muttered looking at the ground in shame. Well that certainly let him know what she was like she thought. I couldn't have made more of a spectacle of myself, they even had to stop the chairlift for a few minutes.

"Ciao" she heard and Carly nudged her as the two Italians sailed passed her waving their poles.

"I think they are at our hotel." said Carly with a familiar glint in her eye." you seem to have made an impression!"

"Don't " said Ellie that was so embarrassing. I hope they aren't at our hotel."

The rest of the lesson went fairly uneventfully and Ellie only fell over once. She thought that she managed to get up again before Dario noticed. She wasn't keen on following each other in a line, she was always worried that she would knock someone over. Also she liked to hang at the back as she found that she went a bit faster than the others and would catch them up. If she delayed starting off it seemed to work, although it probably meant that she had no control.

There was an older man called Don in the group who was not quite so good as the rest of the group and appeared to have a problem stopping, He skied almost straight down the slope and was heading towards a tree. Dario set off in hot pursuit and managed to head him off. Ellie noticed that Dario was very patient with him and subtly nudged one of the group out of the way at the next chairlift so that he could sit by Don and talk to him. He was quite a character and made Dario laugh.

They stopped at a bar on the slope halfway through the lesson. Ellie had a hot chocolate as she thought anything alcoholic would make her worse. They all sat on bench tables outside and warmed up in the sunshine. Ellie had got quite cold standing at the side of the slope while Dario demonstrated parallel turns. Two older couples in the group were talking to Dario and asked him to sit with them. He glanced over at Ellie and Carly a couple of times, at least Ellie thought he did it was hard to tell when he was wearing sun glasses. Ellie had taken the opportunity to take off her helmet and shake her hair loose as the strap needed adjusting. Really these helmets weren't the most flattering things , she thought.

Ellie started to enjoy the lesson as she began to get her ski legs. She was smiling to herself as she rounded a bend and saw that Dario had stopped to help Don, he smiled at Ellie.
"Very good, try not to move the shoulders when you turn."
Ellie concentrated on this for the rest of the lesson. As usual when she concentrated she pulled a face. At the end of the lesson Dario asked her if she had enjoyed the lesson as she looked 'tense'. Once again she looked an idiot as she looked at him vacantly until she realised what he meant.
"I've been asking Dario the best places to go. I also told him your proper name " Carly bubbled "He said I have a very good position. I really enjoyed that, did you?"
Ellie smiled tightly and walked over to help Mel who had dropped one of her skis.
"How did you get on?" she asked Mel

"Oh don't ask, I was hopeless. I kept falling over. Those slopes are really steep you know. We had a lovely instructor called Alberto but he's getting on. I was worried he would put his back out. I think I've ruined any chances with Max."

"me and you both" muttered Ellie

Mel explained that she had watched ski Sunday on the television and so she thought she had to try and ski straight down and not across the slope. The instructor told her to go and so she started to go straight down, picked up speed and then tried to stop and managed to sit on the back of her skis, which made her go faster and then she demolished another beginners class that was waiting at the bottom.

"honestly I was so embarrassed and it took the other group ages to get back up as they were all tangled up and wobbly on their legs. They were really nice about it though . There was a woman watching and I am sure she filmed it. I will probably become a youtube sensation." she groaned putting her head ins her hands. Ellie laughed

"Don't worry, things will get better. I managed to knock down two men earlier."

Ellie and Mel joined the others at a mountain restaurant for lunch. It was a wooden chalet type building with a log fire and self service restaurant and stunning views. There were people sunning themselves outside on deckchairs. Will, Kate, Gemma and Mark had opted out of lessons as they were all good skiers and had explored the slopes together. Italy was a good choice as lessons only took place in the mornings and not all day. After lunch they all decided to ski down a gentle slope together so that Mel and Max could join them, but Mel insisted on staying.

"I'm hopeless I will only spoil it for the rest of you. I'll stop here for a while and have a lovely hot chocolate" she waved them off " go on shoo "

After a while Ellie decided to go back to Mel

"Come on drink this."

"What is It?" questioned Mel

"It's called vin brulee , it's mulled wine. I need it, I'm really cold and it will relax you. I'm taking you back to the hotel."

"Great'" beamed Mel "Mmmm this is great , it's warming my cockles."

Outside Ellie instructed Mel to put her skis on.

"but can't I just walk to the chairlift?"

"No because we are going to ski down."

"No I can meet you at the bottom."

"put on your skis " instructed Ellie firmly

Mel clipped on her skis with Ellie's help and Ellie led her to the top of the slope. Mel shrieked with terror, looked down the slope, started to slide down backwards and ended up in a heap at the side of the piste. It took Ellie and a passing German quite a while to get her back on her feet

"Now listen " Ellie instructed her sternly "You are panicking. You had a few goes on the indoor slope at home so you know how to snow plough. Now follow me, we are going to stop every few minutes and I want you to watch me not the slope.You don't have to go straight down, we can keep going across the slope."

Ellie went slowly and stopped after a few minutes. Mel was frowning in concentration with her eyes fixed on Ellie, she was bent down and quite rigid.

"Great you are doing really well, now lets do the next bit and try to relax. "

Mel relaxed slightly and wiggled her shoulders, although she never took her eyes off Ellie. They skied across the slope , turning in a wide curve at the edges . They finally got to the bottom.

" Now turn around and look . You see you have done it and you haven't fallen over once."

"I can't believe I just did that" exclaimed Mel looking back up the mountain and beaming " Thanks Ellie I feel so much happier now. I think I will be O.K. tomorrow, maybe I should have mulled wine with my breakfast !"

Ellie sat down to take off her boots. She found Melissa red faced and struggling with her boots. Ellie helped her pull them of.

"Oooh the relief" sighed Mel as the first boot came off "that's better than an orgasm, oooh and another" as the second boot came off. She wriggled her toes happily and the Italian man sitting opposite smirked.

"Right then let's go for a shower, now you have had your orgasms of course." she grinned looking at Mel's ski boots. The others called them from the bar and they joined them for a quick drink.

That evening after dinner they all went to another hotel which had a disco. It was great crunching along in the snow together, wearing comfortable boots. The air felt really cold on their faces and Ellie was glad of her woolly hat. The music was really good, mixed with a bit of europop which Ellie loved. She was soon dancing away wildly when she noticed Dario leaning against the bar watching her. He smiled and Ellie pretended she hadn't seen him and carried on dancing. Why was she always so embarrassed when she met someone she really liked ? When she looked again Dario had gone. Ellie could dance for hours . Carly was fighting a losing battle with Piero the snowboard instructor, he was charming and paid her attention and danced with her, but he also paid attention to and danced with about six other women. The others shouted to say they were leaving so Ellie and Carly grabbed their jackets and followed.

The following morning Ellie found that she was skiing quite well and decided she would be brave and try and sit by Dario on the chairlift. Carly or Don kept pipping her to the post so she decided not to bother. Dario informed them that they were going on a different chairlift with a moving floor. "Now I 'ope you can all manage. I will get on last to see you all get on. I think you 'ad better get on with me Ellee as you had problems yesterday, yes?"

Ellie nodded in shame and watched the others leave. When it was their turn Dario grabbed her firmly and they both sat down together. It was wonderful, Dario chatted to her pointing out different mountains and telling her about all the different animals that had made their paw prints in the snow. Ellie felt herself relax and chatted back. Thankfully it was a long ride. Dario asked if Ellie had a boyfriend . She replied that she hadn't at the moment , but didn't dare ask if he had a girlfriend. Anyway she kept reminding herself that she wasn't interested. She asked why his English was so good and he explained that he worked in a tourist resort on the coast in the summer, which had a lot of english speaking visitors.

"It would be very boring to stay 'ere in the summer . We have many people who like to walk and climb the mountains though. Do you like climbing the mountains ? "

Ellie shook her head in horror

" I have enough trouble climbing on and off a chairlift."

he laughed

"You are not so bad . "

" I am a bit accident prone " confessed Ellie. He didn't understand what she meant so she told him the soup story as an example . He was still laughing when he helped off the lift. He seemed a bit self conscious of the scar running down one side of his face and tried to turn that side of his face away. She liked faces with character and so she thought it made him look even better, a bit like a swashbuckling pirate. When Dario had grabbed her arm as the chairlift reached the top Ellie had felt an electric shock pass through her and nearly fell over again.

Ellie watched him ski over to the others. "Steady girl." she breathed remember your resolution
"Yes ,but he's gorgeous and not how you thought he would be" a little voice inside her head insisted.

At the end of the lesson he walked over to her .
" You like music?" he asked
Ellie said that she loved music.
"There is a band tonight at the bar in centre of the village. They are very good, my friend he play guitar. You tell your friends."
Ellie nodded happily and tried to act cool.

The gang all met up again for lunch and this time Mel joined them for a gentle ski, she did well and then a snow boarder came up behind her and caught her ski, she promptly fell over. After that if she heard a snow boarder coming she would stop and wait for them to go past.
" Snow boarders can be a bit more out of control sometimes" said Gemma but they are responsible for going around you as the person in front has priority. Just don't stop suddenly as they won't be expecting that."
Mel whimpered and she and Max decided to go for a drink while the others tackled more difficult slopes. After a while Ellie decided that she had had enough for one day and was walking through the resort when she spotted Mel in the window of a bar with a huge slice of cake in front of her. Mel waved frantically and Ellie went and joined her.
" you have to try this cake, it's the best thing ever " groaned Mel. It was some sort of chocolatey creation and Ellie couldn't resist ordering one for herself , with a flavoured hot chocolate.
" you were right " she grinned wiping her mouth
" you've missed a bit ' pointed Mel. Ellie asked how things were going with Max
"I don't know" she confided . " Max seems to like me but doesn't seem to notice me. If you know what I mean. After we skied down I said I was coming here and he said he was going back up the slope to practise. I was hoping that he would come with me."
"I think you need to make him a bit jealous then he would notice you."
"Oh I couldn't do that. I'm hopeless at flirting."
" Me too. We should ask Carly for lessons."

The two men who had helped Ellie up on her first day said hello to them on their way into the hotel. Ellie groaned Carly had been correct. They seemed very pleasant though.

"Hello you two, how are you getting on?" Gemma and Mark waved to them from the bar. Ellie told them about the band and they all agreed to give it a try. Ellie had another warming glass of vin brûlée and they all sat around the fire chatting and sharing their adventures from the slopes.

" I love skiing holidays" thought Ellie, everyone seemed so much friendlier than on summer holidays. " Except maybe the smug marrieds " she added as the smug marrieds peered into the bar and shook their heads, tutted a bit and walked away. They always jogged up the stairs instead of taking the lift.

It was amazing how comfy the bed was after a days skiing. Time for a late afternoon nap. Ellie snuggled down with her book and felt her eyes close. She woke an hour later and reluctantly got out of bed. She showered, washed her hair and then looked at her clothes. It was difficult to dress up when you only had jeans to choose from. Ellie decided on a bright red top that suited her colouring and then covered it with her best fleecy cream jumper, she put on her favourite boots, although she would have to put on her moon boots when they went out after dinner. She would be on the floor within seconds if she tried to wear those outside. They met by the cosy log fire and Maria brought them snacks to go with their pre dinner drinks, it was so relaxing Ellie sighed and closed her eyes , bliss.

"these garlicky nibbles are amazing , do you want one ? " Mel was holding the plate out to her Ellie shook her head " I daren't after that huge chocolate cake you forced on me. I am not sure I will have room for dinner. "

" Lightweight " grinned Max helping himself.

They all sat around the same table in the dining room and could choose between soup of the day or pasta of the day, then they had the meat course. Finally they had creme brûlée followed by some little pieces of cheese.

"mmm this red wine is delicious ' said Ellie topping up her glass.

"do you think it is true that we don't put any weight on if we are skiing" Mel whispered " as I am absolutely stuffed. I don't think I should have had that cake, but all this fresh air makes me
 hungry. "

" I am sure it must be true, just think of all the exercise we have been doing " replied Ellie smiling sleepily. They all nipped up to their rooms after dinner to get their jackets, amid much grunting and groaning, as their bruises and stiffness were starting to come out. Ellie jumped in the lift with Mel, who was looking lovely in a black fitted jumper and black jeans.
" I am hoping they make me look slimmer"
" you look lovely, you will have all the Italians after you."
" I would prefer Max " sighed Mel dreamily. Goodness she had got it bad.

"Hey Ellie, here" yelled Carly from across the bar. Ellie grabbed Mel on the way across as Carly was talking to the two Italians who had helped her at the chairlift.
"Aah the ladies 'oo like to lie in the snow." grinned the smaller of the two who had a little goatee beard. Ellie looked at Mel who shrugged
"They have kindly helped me up about ten times in the last two days. I don't think you need to go to the gym with me around." she blushed
"It is no problem we like to 'elp the beautiful ladies." goatee smiled, holding Mel's hand and gazing into her eyes. Meanwhile Carly was flirting outrageously with Gennaro the other 'helper'.
The girls chatted to goatee who admitted he had a wife and two children in Milan. He had come away with his brother for a 'white week' as the Italians called it. He was a born flirt but good fun and the girls enjoyed themselves . Mel relaxed when she realised that he was just flirting. They told him about the band and he asked if he and his brother could join them as it looked as if their group was having a lot of fun. Ellie thought that sounded like a good idea .

The cold night air soon woke them up. "Ooh the cold goes right through these jeans." Gemma complained linking her arms with Mark and Ellie. "What's the matter with Max, he's got a face like thunder?"
Ellie glanced around and Max certainly looked grim. He was glaring at Goatee, who had lifted a giggling Mel over a large pile of snow. Ellie smiled, it looked as though her advice had worked, even if Mel didn't realise.
"no no put me down " shrieked Mel "not here " she yelped when goatee paused over another pile of snow.

Mark said he had spoken to the office and they were doing fine without them. He thought the two had come in to help were enjoying themselves. They had also tidied up the stationary cupboard which had been on Ellie's to do list for ages.

"Are you sure this is the right bar?" queried Mark.
The bar certainly looked a bit quiet. There were two men sitting talking and waving their arms about and that was it. It looked like a 70's bar with bright pink lights over the stage and lino on the floor. Everyone was looking a bit doubtful.
"I am sure he said Bar Lupo " Ellie asked the barman if there was a band playing tonight.
"Sure they will be 'ere soon. You want drinks I make special Bombadino drink."
"Ooh I've heard they are really good" shrieked Kate "we'll all have one". Will rolled his eyes, it looked as if Kate was determined to go on one of her benders. She was well known for drinking loads and being the life and soul of the party and then suddenly disappearing. It once took Will three hours to find her fast asleep in someone's front garden. The drink was bright yellow with cream on top. It was delicious but a little sickly. Ellie ordered a coke next as with the wine at dinner and the pre dinner drink, she had already drunk quite a lot. Not to mention the vin brûlées.

They had a couple of drinks and it was still quiet. " I am not sure that I can stay up late " groaned Mel " I am soo tired . I thought we would all be partying 'til the early hours, but we are all ready for bed by ten !."
" Come on you will be fine. Look I think goatee is waving you over."
Mel tripped across the floor and Max stood glaring at goatee and then joined them to ask if they wanted drinks. He returned with the drinks and pushed his way in next to Mel, elbowing goatee out of the way.

Ellie kept glancing around but there was no sign of Dario. Some more people had wandered in. At least the band had arrived and were messing about with their instruments and someone had put some music on the speakers, so they decided to have a dance.
 " After all we don't know anyone, so we can let ourselves go. Why are you buying that man drinks? I'm sure I have seen him before." she frowned.
The man was an Italian in his fifties, with a black and grey moustache and bushy eyebrows. He raised his wineglass at Mel and smiled.

"Oh that's Luca, he's the man from the main chairlift, he is lovely. I fell off the seat when I tried to use it the first time. He stopped the lift and helped me on. Now when he sees me coming he slows down the lift and helps me on, so I bought him a drink. " Mel waved at him and went to join the others on the dance floor. Ellie shrugged and joined her, only Mel would do that she smiled. After dancing for half an hour she stopped for a breather and a coke.

"Mel wants to be careful," Ellie looked up and saw Max frowning in the direction of Mel and Carly who were now sitting with the brothers. "He looks like a right Romeo and she will only get upset. You know how sensitive she is."

"Oh I think Mel can take care of herself, he's really nice and he looks out for Mel when she is skiing and helps her out." They hadn't told Max that goatee was married.

Max went off muttering just as Dario came through the door with some of the other instructors. He looked fantastic in his jeans and a tight jumper . He was quite skinny but Ellie liked skinny men, he still had muscles, probably from pulling up people like me she thought.

"Hi so you 'ave come to see the band."

Ellie nodded " I was worried, I thought we had the wrong place. We have been here ages. "

"Oh no it is too early yet. Relax we are in Italy. We start quite late and the band finish second set about one a.m."

"Wow " said Ellie " I thought that this was a quiet little village., I don't think we will be able to stay awake that late." Dario smiled

" You need siesta in afternoon."

"One bombadino" Kate plonked another bright yellow drink on the table .

Dario raised an eyebrow "You need to be careful with those, they are very good , but very strong." He strolled over to join his friends.

"Anyone for another bombadino" shouted Max. Ellie shook her head, she didn't want to make a fool of herself, she knew that Italians rarely got drunk and considered that it ruined their image if they did so.

'Woo woo ' Max, Gemma, Kate and Mark had their arms around each other and were dancing madly to the band. Will was leaning against the bar chatting to one of the ski instructors. Ellie was dancing with Mel and some others, while Carly was ensconced in the corner with Gennaro from their hotel. Ellie loved the band, she and Sam had really got into music when Rick was in the band and they still went to see live music whenever they could. Ellie then danced with some of the ski instructors and locals. Dario appeared to enjoy the band, but remained at the bar. Ellie sat down to have a drink, brushing her sweaty hair off her face and Dario walked over.

"You are enjoying the band?'

"They are great" beamed Ellie

"Your friends they have left."

Ellie glanced around and could only see Carly and Gennaro in the corner "Oh I didn't realise. I'm a bit of a night owl and I love to dance."

Dario looked a bit confused at the 'night owl'

"I mean I like to go to bed late. I'm not so good in the morning."

"Oh I understand now why you fall over in my lesson."

"Cheeky" Ellie poked him in the ribs. They sat listening to the band and chatting about music. Ellie discovered they had similar tastes. She told him about Rick's band and how they used to help him with the lyrics. The band finished and started to pack up. Ellie looked around and discovered that even Carly had left, she put on her ski jacket and said goodbye to Dario. He smiled at her and when she got outside she realised he had followed her.

"I will take you back to 'otel"

"No I'm fine honestly." she stuttered

Dario smiled at her, linked arms and proceeded to give her a guided tour of the resort on the way back. Ellie hoped they wouldn't find Kate in a heap in the snow. They stood at the top of the nursery slope and looked down the mountain at the twinkling lights of the villages below.

"It's so beautiful" breathed Ellie "You are very lucky living here."

Dario shrugged "It is very beautiful in the winter, but in the summer not so good, so I go and work in a bar at the 'ow you say 'seaside?"

Ellie nodded, she was quickly losing the power of speech, she could feel his arm next to hers and felt as though little electric shocks were running up and down her arm. She asked the name of the seaside resort and discovered that it was on the island of Elba in Tuscany near a place she had visited several times with her parents. Her whole family loved Italy and in particular Elba as it had beautiful beaches . He was pleased that she knew about it. He said that he helped out in his uncle's bar.

" so you speak Italian then if you come 'ere for your 'olidays ? Not many English people visit Elba, is usually German people .I no need to speak English!"

" no need at all if you want me to order a meal or a drink but I am not much good with anything else. It's awful us Brits should be ashamed ."

" I teach you then " and he picked up Ellie's hand, covered in her woolly mittens " mano is hand, now you repeat."

"Mano" said Ellie faintly . He continued to hold her hand and point out other objects, making her repeat the words. Dario explained that in the winter season he often had to work seven days a week. Sometimes he had some free time in the afternoon, if he did not have a private lesson. Changeover days were usually taken up with private lessons, as it was the weekend and a lot of Italians drove up for the day. He asked her about her village and she described the pretty High street with the church and pub.

"Oh yes I would like to try English pub. I went to London once with school but was not allowed in pubs. " he smiled. Ellie thought she would love to show him an English pub, her heart was racing and every time she looked at him she felt a tingling sensation all over.

He asked if she had any brothers or sisters and she told him about her younger brother Andrew who used to tease her, but was now at university studying to be a lawyer. Dario said that he was an only child but had grown up with lots of friends in the village.

They arrived at the hotel and Dario turned her to face him "buonanotte beautiful Ellee " and gently kissed her. Ellie threaded her fingers through his hair and kissed him back. She felt as though she was spinning around and around and then falling into a big void and wanted the kiss to go on forever. They parted breathlessly and Ellie looked at him dazedly, Dario looked a bit shaken .

"I see you tomorrow Ellee." and he was gone .

Dario shook his head as he walked home. What just happened there! He mostly went out with local girls and sometimes had fun with tourists , particularly in the summer, but he had never felt a kiss like that before.

Ellie stumbled up to bed, she had never ever felt like that when she had kissed someone, she hadn't even recovered her power of speech to say bye. He was just so perfect , he was handsome, sexy and kind. He probably thought that she had never been kissed before, the way she had reacted.

"I bet he kisses a different girl every week that is why he is so good." she thought and then smiled as she drifted off to sleep, perhaps a holiday romance would do her good but she had better be careful, she didn't want a broken heart.

CHAPTER SIX

The following morning there were a few sore heads at breakfast . Will and Kate arrived late and appeared to be having a row. Gemma said that they often had rows and sometimes thought that they weren't suited for each other. The smug marrieds shot them disapproving looks as they left. When they all walked up towards the lift, they had to stop for Kate to be sick at the side of the road., which annoyed Will.

"Why don't you ever learn ." he snarled.

They quickly covered it up with a pile of snow. The older group walked past as they were doing it.

" Don't worry" shouted one of them "we've all been there."

"except the smug marrieds" muttered Will glaring at Kate.

"Morning everyone" Dario smiled at the class. Ellie smiled shyly, she was determined to play it cool, but couldn't help blushing. The kiss probably meant nothing to him. Carly managed to sit by Dario on the chairlift and Ellie made no attempt to stop her. Dario sat by her on the last chairlift to the top before the end of the lesson.

"Are you Ok?" he questioned looking at Ellie uncertainly. Ellie smiled brightly

" Yes of course"

" Good. I have to go and see my grandfather who is in hospital tonight, but would you have drink with me tomorrow night?" Ellie agreed and he explained that his grandfather Alfreddo, who had grown up in the village was very ill in hospital.

"He was an instructor like me and I am very close to him. My father he did not want to be an instructor and he move away to become a farmer. My grandparents live with my parents in the countryside now and my grandfather he give me 'is house here. He 'as not been well for long time but now I am very worried. " Dario looked genuinely upset and Ellie felt her heart go out to him.

"Then you must go. I expect he likes to hear all the news from the village. He must be very proud of you. "

Dario nodded sadly. Ellie chatted to him about her family to distract him and made him laugh when she told him about her dad's elderberry wine. Although he was a little confused that wine could be made of something called an elderberry.

" What is elderberry Ellee ?"

Ellie noticed that he treated Carly politely but did not encourage her, although he was an incorrigible flirt with the other women in the class, particularly the older ones. She had seen him teaching a group of very small children and he was brilliant with them. When everyone met for lunch Ellie noticed that Max was carrying Mel's skis and Mel was blushing madly. They insisted that they would ski together in the afternoon and give the others a chance to try the more difficult slopes. Carly was going skiing with Goatee's brother Gennaro as it was his last day, so goatee joined them. Max put his arm around Mel protectively and led her off to the gentle slope, giving goatee a dirty look over his shoulder. Earlier Ellie had noticed him swapping goatee's skis for another pair that looked similar.

Everyone set off and Ellie and goatee were last. Ellie was struggling with some ice on her bindings and had forgotten about the skis until goatee fell over trying to put on his skis and said his ski settings were too big and didn't fit his boots.

"someone 'as taken the wrong skis" he roared and stamped over to the rack. Ellie helped him find the right skis whilst trying not to laugh. He was most indignant and kept saying

"oo 'as done this to me"

As they skied down together she noticed Dario leaning out of a chairlift peering down at her. She was not as good as Gemma, Mark, Kate and Will but she managed to keep up with them, so she was quite proud of her skiing. Kate was still looking a bit green and had sworn never to drink again.

Ellie decided to finish before the others as her legs were tired. There was no Mel to have a hot chocolate with so she mooched around the pretty shops. There were lots of gorgeous things that wouldn't fit in a suitcase. There was a tiny gift shop decorated with pine branches and twinkly lights around the door. The Christmas decorations were reduced and Ellie couldn't resist a tiny pair of wooden skis to hang on the Christmas tree. A cute little gonk with the name of the resort was next and she bought another two for her mom and dad and Sam. All of Ellie's family adored Christmas and Sam always decorated her tree beautifully. This year however Ralph had decided that they would have a minimalist tree in black which had looked awful. The gonk would probably not be allowed . When she came out of the shop she saw a woman standing by the window. She glared at Ellie. Ellie looked behind but couldn't see anyone else. She frowned, the woman was wearing a ski instructor jacket but Ellie didn't remember seeing her before. Ellie looked in some ski wear shops but the clothes were very expensive. She had been thinking about buying her own ski boots as if she went skiing several times she would soon get her money back. Gemma and Mark had their own ski boots and said they were far more comfortable. Mel had found her boots a bit tight and had gone back to the hire shop to swap them. One pastry shop had the most beautiful tiramisu cake in the fridge in the window. Ellie was trying to think if it was anyone's birthday as she would love an excuse to buy it.

When she got back to the bar the others were having a drink and asked if they had seen Mel and Max as the light was starting to go and they were getting concerned.
" They are probably having a cheeky hot chocolate somewhere ." replied Ellie 'although I have walked all through the village and haven't seen them."
Later Will was demonstrating a skiing incident when a bedraggled frozen looking Mel and Max appeared. They quickly made room for them by the fire and got them vin brûlées. Mel couldn't stop her teeth chattering for a while.
"What on earth happened. " asked Kate kneeling by Mel and rubbing her hands.
"we got a bit lost." replied Max. "We were doing well with our skiing and thought we would try a slope we had been on in our lesson. Turns out it wasn't that slope , so we took off our skis and slid and walked along the edge of the slope. Then we weren't sure where we were when we got to the bottom. It's taken ages to get back as we have had to slide down a lot of slopes. We could even see a snow plough in the distance so we knew that the last slope we were on had closed. "
" It was awful " Mel said " thank goodness for Max because I was really scared and he looked after me. He carried my skis for most of the way."
Max hugged her and kissed he top of her head.
" It hasn't put you off skiing has it ? " Ellie asked anxiously
They both shook their heads
" We are just going to stick to the slopes we know in future ." replied Max
" I have just realised " said Mel " we were so worried we didn't even stop for a hot chocolate ! I have missed my afternoon hot chocolate."
" You are getting back to normal then. " smiled Gemma

They were all shattered that night and decided to stop around the fire , play games and have an early night. There was a humming game which was hilarious as Max couldn't hum and made a strange noise down his nose. They were all crying with laughter as Max , red in the face kept repeating the same strange noise and telling them that they all knew the tune, he also did the moves to the music he was humming.

" You know this one it's always played at discos " he said with exasperation. Enzo added another large log to the fire and stayed to watch . He called Maria and they joined in the laughter. Charades was next which was also funny, as Enzo decided to join in and there was some confusion between the two cultures. He did act out 'Jaws" but Ellie had never seen a shark like Enzo's. He kept trying to attack different people and Ellie had tears rolling down her face laughing at the expression on his face. Gemma's Sound of Music was also something to behold.

They all went to bed just after ten.

"ooh did you hear my knee creak then? " said Ellie, holding on to the handrail and pulling herself up the stairs. She was regretting telling Mel and Max to go in the tiny lift as the stairs seem to be going on forever.

" I will need another holiday after this " she puffed

" We must be getting old" exclaimed Gemma " we should be partying 'til dawn."

" It was that late night last night " said Mark planting a kiss on Gemma's cheek.

"Aren't Mel and Max getting on well." observed Gemma " I am so pleased for her, she is a lovely girl. I'm pleased for you too " she added nudging Ellie.

" He is lovely but I am not raising my hopes ." replied Ellie "goodnight or should I say buona notte."

Ellie couldn't wait to get into her pyjamas, she snuggled into bed and started to read her book. She loved her cosy room and comfortable bed, she was only on page twenty and that was what she had read on the plane. Her eyes started to droop after a page and a half.

The following morning they were all keen to get on the slopes. Ellie's group had to ski holding their ski poles across their body and Ellie and Carly were both concentrating on the exercise so much that they carried on way past Dario and joined another ski group. Dario was helping Don extricate himself from some shrubbery at the side of the slope.

"Hey come back you two, you no like my class no more ? "

They both got a fit of the giggles when they realised what they had done.

Ellie felt she had really improved and was enjoying herself. Dario had skied up to her and asked casually who the Italian with the goatee was and said she should be careful. Ellie replied that he was just a friend from the hotel , he had a wife and she did not like goatees or beards at which Dario rubbed his stubble reflectively.

" He seemed jealous " smiled Ellie gleefully.

Dario joined them for a drink at a local bar in the evening. She noticed one of the women ski instructors glaring at her, it was the same woman she had seen outside the shop.
"who's that woman?"
"oh that ees Gabriella she new here this season and we have been helping her settle in. She keep asking me for help. She very nice to me but I not sure I like her. She was how you say, mean to Ariana one of the other instructors and I saw her shout at a small boy and make 'im cry yesterday. I found him later and give 'im sweets and tell 'im not to worry."
"well if looks could kill" thought Ellie. Mind you she couldn't blame her, Dario was looking fabulous tonight , his black wavy hair curled over his collar, but something was different. Ellie peered at him more closely and noticed that his stubble had gone. He looked good in everything he wore, Italians all seemed to have so much style.
Gabriella was stick thin with dark hair tied in a ponytail and mean looking eyes, which she fluttered at Dario whenever he spoke to her, she would also place her hand on his arm. He chatted to Ellie's friends and made them laugh telling the story of the woman in his beginners class last year who was so scared of getting off the chairlift that she left it until the lift turned around at the top and started to go down.
" she was danglin' off lift . They stop it but I 'ad to run an' try an' catch her. She big woman an' fell on top of me. I 'ad black eye. Another time my class had to go on how you say, button lift ? One man 'e was 'opeless . He kept falling off an' I 'ad to 'elp 'im down an' he would try again. on tenth time I thought 'e got it 'e was 'alf way up then 'e wobble. Dio mio 'e come back down backwards."
They laughed and Mark offered him another drink
" No grazie I take the lovely Ellee somewhere private with me " and he winked at them. Ellie blushed scarlet. He helped her on with her jacket and waved goodbye.
"eek there she goes again. " thought Ellie as Gabriella glared at her and then turned her back to them.

He took Ellie to a quiet bar at the other end of the village. They chatted and Ellie found he was interested in lots of things and was very knowledgable. He was quite serious at times, although they laughed about a few things. He was genuinely interested when she told him about her job at the estate agents.

" Maybe you could do that 'ere in Italy " he said.

"Maybe but I would have to learn Italian first."

Ellie found herself telling him about Sam and Ralph.

" 'e no sound like right person for your friend " he frowned " bring her 'ere and I find 'er nice Italian man. Like me " he smirked at Ellie

" Oh I couldn't do that to the poor girl " laughed Ellie . At which Dario picked up an ice cube and threatened to put it down Ellie's jumper. He was still trying to get her when they walked outside. Ellie raced ahead.

" Dario, Dario "

Ellie turned around and saw two small children run at Dario.

" Roberto , Silvia " and he picked them up and swung them around , amid much giggling. He pretended to throw them into the pile of snow.

" now go to your papa 'e is waiting." The children hugged him and ran off, Silvia blowing kisses as she ran.

" looks like you have a few more fans " smiled Ellie

" oh they lovely children I teach them to ski since they very little.They live 'ere. "

He chatted to her about his grandfather and on the way back he showed her 'Alfreddo's house' as he called it.

"It is not big 'ouse but I no need big 'ouse , so is fine,"

Ellie thought it looked really cute like a little Swiss music box. She tried not to touch Dario as she walked along as every time they touched she felt an electric shock jolt through her. They stood looking down at the twinkling lights and Dario kissed her again. The kiss seemed to go on forever and Ellie felt herself melt. When they drew apart her legs felt wobbly. What was happening to her, she had never felt like this before. Dario gazed into her eyes and gently touched her face

"Cara Ellee I like you very much. I 'ave to go to the "ospital again tomorrow, but I go in the afternoon as I 'ave no lessons. Will you come to my 'ouse tomorrow night and I will cook for you ?"

Ellie hesitated ,she felt she was getting in too deep and too quickly. She was going home on Saturday and didn't want to leave with a broken heart.

"What is the matter?"

"nothing"

"there is something what is it ? You no like me ? "

"no it's not that , its ,its just that you are Italian .."

"Si" he shrugged

"and you are a ski instructor"

"si"

"and well you are used to seeing lots and lots of girls here and at the seaside and you will have forgotten me by next week. I, I don't jump into bed with lots of different men you know."

Dario smiled

"I know Ellee" he gently stroked her face "That is why I like you, you are interesting and funny and help people. You are not like other girls I meet who are on 'oliday. Come on I make you nice meal. What is your favourite food? "

Ellie shook her head " I don't know .."

" come on you not know what you like to eat ?"

" No it's not that …"

Dario bent his head and smiled and batted his eyelashes at her. How could she resist those brilliant blue eyes.

" Oh O.K. Spaghetti ? "

"Spaghetti easy I can do that and.."

"and tiramisu " said Ellie hopefully

Dario chuckled " You like tiramisu ? My nonna ,that is my grandmother, she make best tiramisu in the world. I get her to make one, my father he is giving me how you say , a food box from my momma tomorrow at the 'ospital. She think I not eat enough " he grinned. " Also with my grandfather so ill they all like to keep busy."

Ellie smiled and nodded. She couldn't help herself, her heart soared when she saw him and even if she was miserable when she got home, it would have been worth it. Life was too short to pass by someone as fantastic as Dario.

" I hope your grandfather is O.K. It must be a very worrying time for your family."

Dario nodded sadly " 'e is getting weaker every time I see 'im. I no think 'e will get better." and he kissed her goodnight sadly. Ellie sat in her bedroom gazing out of the window for ages and thinking about Dario. Maybe she could go to Italian lessons and get a job at an estate agents. It couldn't be much different and she was quite good at taking photos. She had noticed that the Italian agents didn't always take a photo of the outside of a house and would just show a photo of a fireplace or something. Walkers came here in the summer, but she didn't think it was likely that there were many properties for sale at any time. She jumped into bed thinking of other jobs she could do here. A ski instructor was out, as was a cook, but maybe she could work behind a bar, she would like that.

Ellie woke with a smile on her face. Tonight she was going to be with Dario alone in his house.
"I'm not here for dinner tonight" Ellie informed Maria after breakfast the following day.
"Why you no like my cooking?" Maria tried to look stern
"No I've got a date" muttered Ellie looking sheepish
"oo with ?" demanded Maria
"Dario"
"Oh Dario 'e very good looking but 'e nice boy. 'ow is Alfreddo?"
"He is still quite ill I think."
Maria walked off shaking her head sadly. The others teased Ellie
" Who has a hot date " Gemma shouted " could it be that person who said she was off men and would certainly steer clear of Italian men ?"
Ellie shrugged and smiled."What can I say. I was wrong."
"good for you" shouted Carly " I'm not bitter, I have a date with a hot German tonight."
"You don't hang around " whistled Max " that Gennaro has only just left."
"What can I say. I am irresistible " grinned Carly wiggling her bottom on the way to picking up another croissant.

They all seemed to ski well today and Dario only had to retrieve Don from the edge of the slope once.
" Good you should all make me proud at the slalom race tomorrow " beamed Dario
Ellie was a bit concerned about going in and out of the slalom poles as although she was quite fast she was not so good at turning. She would probably be scattering poles all over the place. Carly dashed off at the end of the lesson as she had arranged to meet the new man that she had met, in the mountain restaurant. She certainly didn't do badly.
" I don't know how she does it " thought Ellie " although I am not doing too badly" and she smiled at Dario who had been grabbed by Don. He blew her a kiss.

Ellie had a drink with the others in the hotel before dinner. She felt nervous and there was a piece of hair that kept sticking up. She leaned back to try and see her face in the mirror behind the bar and nearly fell off the stool.

" Whoops " Carly grabbed her " Calm down you look great . Just enjoy. I tried, but he only had eyes for you. Come on I will walk with you. I am meeting that German in a restaurant in the village, he is taking me to dinner. They walked arm in arm up to the village and Carly made her laugh about her plans for the German

" you are incorrigible " laughed Ellie

" yes but I know how to have a good time. Make sure you do too." and she blew a kiss at Ellie and marched purposely towards the restaurant.

Ellie scrunched on past a few shops and a bar until she came to Alfreddo's house. She tapped lightly on the door, suddenly feeling shy. The house was a lovely old stone house, joined on either side by similar houses. It had shutters at the windows and was quite pretty. The door was enormous and made of really old wood, with a great big knocker. She tried to use the knocker but was struggling with it when the door shot open and a grinning Dario appeared.

"wow you are looking very 'ot " whistled Dario when she shrugged off her coat "come and sit by the fire." Ellie had put on a lovely blue top , which matched her eyes and brushed her hair until it gleamed.

Dario was only wearing jeans and a white long sleeved T shirt but he looked amazing.

The red wine glinted in the firelight and Ellie took tiny sips, she was determined to keep her wits about her. Dario whistled in the kitchen. The house looked very tidy, the walls were painted white and lovely old beams ran across the ceiling. There was a lovely old fireplace with a basket of logs at the side.There were books and cds scattered about but it felt homely, with a lovely squishy sofa. Ellie stood up to look at some framed photos of his family and an old photo of a grinning young man holding a pair of wooden skis. This must be his beloved grandfather Alfreddo, Ellie could see a resemblance, except his grandfather was sporting an impressive moustache. She looked at the other photos trying to guess which were his parents. Ellie was looking through the CD's which were mostly quite old , while music was playing in the background. She heard a europop one she had liked at the bar the other night and started tapping her foot, then as no one was around she had a little dance. She heard the sound of a throat being cleared and spun around.

"Dinner is ready" grinned Dario

Ellie blushed and sat down. Sometimes she couldn't help herself, she must stop it. He had made an effort with the table, it was carefully laid with a huge candle surrounded by greenery flickering in the centre. Dario looked so gorgeous in the candlelight that she forgot to eat for a moment.

The spaghetti was fantastic, Ellie had a good appetite and she always felt hungry after a day on the slopes. Dario watched her demolish the pasta with a grin.

"I think you must be Italian" he said standing up to top up her glass. " I like girls who eat, not very thin girls like Gabriella." Then he leant over and kissed her gently and slowly. Ellie felt lust flood over her. She entwined her hands in his hair and kissed him passionately, she was on fire.

"oh Ellee you are so beautiful." murmured Dario. He lifted her off the chair and they staggered to the rug in front of the fire and started tearing clothes off each other . Dario was muttering endearments in Italian whilst looking deep into her eyes . Ellie was drowning and everything was spiralling out of control.

Finally they lay sated in front of the fire.

Dario tucked Ellie's hair behind her ear and kissed her gently.

"Ellee I know you think I 'ave lots of women but I 'ave never felt like this before. I love you."

"I love you too"

They lay gazing at each other. Ellie traced her finger along his scar and then kissed it.

" I love your scar, how did you get it ? "

"You like my scar ? You are weird girl !"

He explained that it was from a skiing accident when he was a child. He had ignored his grandfather's instructions and skied off piste. He had hit a rock and slammed into the branch of a tree.

" My grandfather he very mad at me."

" Well I love it . One day I would like my friend Sam to paint you."

Dario leant on one elbow " so Sam is artist ?"

Ellie nodded " I wish she felt about Ralph the way I feel about you. I just know she doesn't." suddenly she sat up "tiramisu you never gave me any tiramisu. "

Dario chuckled and returned from the kitchen with two huge bowls of tiramisu. He fed her the first few mouthfuls it was delicious.

"mmmmm" murmered Ellie finally licking her spoon "ten"

"ten what ? " queried Dario.

They curled up in front of the fire together and listened to music and talked. Finally Ellie stretched and yawned.

"I had better get back to the hotel. I have an important race tomorrow."

"yes, you better not fall over an' make me look rubbish teacher" grinned Dario pulling her to him for another passionate kiss. In the end he persuaded her to stay the night and leave early the following morning. It was strange seeing his bedroom . His clothes were carefully hung on a rail and there was a pile of books by the bed.

" I wonder if he has to take emergency books with him " mused Ellie and then she shrieked as Dario ran at her and threw her on the bed. Dario walked her back to the hotel early the next morning " see you later bella " and he kissed her tenderly.

Ellie drifted up to her room in a cloud of happiness. She rang Sam ,which woke Sam as they were still in bed. Ellie could hear Ralph muttering angrily next to Sam

"who the hell is that at this time of day! "

" sorry" whispered Ellie " I just had to tell you. I have met the love of my life and he is wonderful."
Sam had crept into the bathroom and they had a whispered conversation for the next half hour. Sam was thrilled for Ellie. Then Ellie heard Ralph shouting to Sam to

"come back to bed for God's sake. Its six in the morning and I have a meeting later !'

They hurriedly rang off and Ellie tried to snatch some sleep , realising it was an hour later in Italy.

CHAPTER SEVEN

"I can't believe it's our last day " wailed Mel as they were handed bibs for the end of week slalom competition and then she saw the slalom poles

"oh no ! I can't ski round those poles and down the mountain." she shrieked

"you only have to go through the bottom four silly." said Max kissing her fondly.

Ellie grinned at least that was one relationship that would carry on when they got home.

She strolled over to her group "Would you stay with me tonight? I have to pack and should stay in the hotel on my last night " she whispered to Dario

"yes of course I will . I have to go to ski school in the morning but I will come to wave you off and kiss you goodbye. You have my mobile number ? "

"yes and you have mine and we will text each other every day"

"and you will come and stay with me in the summer?"

Ellie nodded happily " I am enrolling for Italian lessons as soon as I get home and

you can come and stay with me in my little flat when the ski season finishes and before the summer season starts."

Dario beamed " yes I would like that very much an' you can take me to pub . Now put on your bib we 'ave a race to do."

The slalom race was fun. It was done like a proper race, with a man at the top with a flag and someone else timing them. They each had a bib with a number on the back. All the classes took part but at different times and with an increasing number of poles to go around , depending on the ability of the class. Although Ellie was not as fast as some of the others, at least she didn't fall over like Carly who was showing off and going really fast. Carly managed to miss one pole and wrap herself in some netting at the side and it took a while for them to disentangle her. She was even beaten by Don who went really slowly but didn't fall over. He had learnt to control his speed under Dario's tuition. Max won the race for the beginners and they were all told to meet at the large hotel near the ski school after dinner for the presentation.

Ellie and Dario managed to have a coffee together. They didn't talk much they just held hands and gazed at each other until one of the other instructors tapped him on the shoulder and said it was time to go. Ellie sat gazing dreamily out of the window until the others appeared to drag her off for a last lunch at the mountain restaurant.

"Stop smiling at the mountains and come and have lunch." said Gemma pulling her off the chair "honestly you have been on another planet all day. It's a wonder you managed the slalom !"

They had panini and shared a huge plate of chips

" I am so going to miss this " groaned Mel dipping her chip into a pool of mayonnaise .

Then they finished with a vin brûlée and skied down the mountain together. A passing skier kindly took a photo of them all with their arms around each other and one ski sticking in the ground.

"Woa we nearly went there " shouted Max as Mel wobbled and nearly knocked over Carly.

"Come on back to my room and help me pack." he smirked at Mel , who blushed furiously . The really good skiers went off for a last ski but the others decided to hand in their equipment and finish. They high fived each other that they had managed the holiday without any broken bones.

" I was going to have a last ski but my legs are really tired and I have heard of people who decide to have a last ski and then break something." said Carly

The others nodded , they had all seen ambulances dashing up to the village throughout the week to collect the unfortunate. Ellie decided to go and pack so that she would have more time to spend with Dario.

They were all in high spirits as they sat down for their last evening meal together and Ellie and Mel compared bruises.

" I don't think I could have skied one more day " said Mel. I ache all over and feel really tired.

"Not too tired to enjoy a last night out though" smiled Max coming up behind Mel and kissing the top of her head. Mel blushed and beamed at Max. Ellie still felt a bit spaced out but it was not surprising as she hadn't had much sleep.

" Well done everyone you have all done really well and we are all in one piece " said Mark. They all nodded and said cheers. One of the smug marrieds had fallen badly on a patch of ice and broken her ankle. Her husband had been heard berating her for persuading them all to do one last ski.

" now we will have to stay a few more days until you are fit to fly and I am supposed to be at work on Monday !" Ellie couldn't help but smile to herself. Not so smug now !

Maria and Enzo brought out free limoncello for all of them at the end of the meal. It was lovely and lemony and very strong and tasted much nicer than the grappa they had tried. All the hotel guests said 'saluti' to each other, except the smug marrieds who had already left the dining room.

"You 'ave all been very nice guests ." smiled Maria "you all come back and see me and Enzo next year , yes ? "

They all nodded and said that they would if they could save enough money.

The whole gang walked through the village to the prize giving. Videos were shown of all the classes, which was a tad embarrassing, although after a few drinks no one cared. They all received a medal from their instructors for completing ski school and trophies were given to the winners of the slalom. The disco then began and Ellie and the gang joined in and Ellie even got Dario to dance. Max danced with his trophy, he had poured his beer in and stopped every so often for a swig . A smoochy song came on and Mel persuaded him to leave it on a table. She was glowing and looked so happy.

After a while Dario took her hand and led her out. They walked slowly through the village, stopping every few minutes to kiss.

" I don't want to go home ." said Ellie clinging to Dario

" I no want you to go home but we will see each other very soon. Yes ?"

Ellie nodded she couldn't believe that they had only known each other for a few days. It felt as if she had always known him.

They spent a glorious last night together talking and making love . Ellie had decided she could sleep when she got home. Ellie trailed her finger over Dario's chest and sighed.

"What's the matter ? You want a muscle man now?" queried Dario , propping himself up on one arm and smiling at her. Ellie shook her head.

"It's just that I didn't mean to come here and fall in love. I was supposed to meet someone in the pub who lived in the Cotswolds. I am going to miss you so much."

"and I will miss you. If you want I come and work in the pub " and he wiggled his eyebrows at her. About seven o'clock in the morning Ellie finally fell asleep in Dario's arms. He lay watching her for a while, then kissed her gently on the forehead. "see you later my beautiful Ellee " and crept out of the room. He switched on his mobile when he got to ski school and frowned when he saw the message. His grandfather had taken a turn for the worse and was not expected to last the day. He quickly scribbled a note for Ellie and looked around. Gabriella was in the tiny kitchen .

"Please give this to Ellee at 'otel Girasole. You know the pretty one with the dark hair and blue eyes? My grandfather he is .." Dario couldn't continue.

"Yes I know her " she smiled putting her arms around Dario "you go to your family. I will take over your private lessons."

"Thanks" Dario smiled gratefully and left. He was so close to his grandfather, who had taught him everything he knew about skiing. He had been so proud when Dario had followed in his footsteps and become an instructor. Although he had been ill for a long time now, it was still a shock . He jumped in his car and raced off down the mountain, tears running down his face.

Ellie's alarm was ringing. She stretched and looked at the space where Dario had lain and felt a wave of sadness . She would not be seeing him for a few months now and phone calls were just not the same. She was determined not to be tearful when he came to say goodbye. He had promised to come and stay with her and she would see him in the summer. She was hoping to go on two holidays to see him if she could wangle it at work. She was determined to come back for skiing next year. She was going to learn Italian too. If things became serious maybe she could work at an estate agents nearby. Whatever it took so that she could be with her soulmate. She was first at breakfast but found she couldn't eat anything. The others clattered down one by one. Most of them looked worse for wear. Ellie sighed and gratefully took the hot chocolate that Maria pressed on her. Maria winked

"you need your strength no ? "

Maria and Enzo waved goodbye to them all and went back into the hotel. Ellie lingered by the back of the coach. All the cases had been loaded. Where was Dario? Some of the instructors walked past and waved to them. Ellie recognised a few of them and called out.

"have you seen Dario ? "

They shook their heads and then Gabriella came over "I think 'e was giving private lesson to that lady with the blond hair. You know what 'e is like, always different ladies . " she smirked and walked off.

Ellie looked at her in horror and then got on the coach . A tear trickled down her face.

"hey " said Carly nudging her "love 'em and leave them that's the way."

"Don't listen to her " whispered Mel " I could tell he really liked you. She is just jealous. Maybe something came up at work." and she hugged Ellie.
Ellie nodded miserably and kept looking back as they drove away. She kept checking her phone every few minutes.

Ellie wasn't with it at the airport, she kept thinking she saw Dario in the crowd and wouldn't join the others at the bar. When their flight was called she didn't get up until the last minute and left her book and mobile on the seat. They had taken off when she looked for her phone and realised what she had done. She informed the airline, but the phone was never seen again. Well she told herself you knew this could happen before you came on holiday. It serves you right.

CHAPTER EIGHT

"I'm really worried about Ellie. I wish I could get hold of that bastard Dario." Gemma whispered to Mark looking over at Ellie's desk.

"I know " replied Mark "she is working too hard, she stays late every night, works every Saturday and she is looking ill. She will be putting the punters off."

"Oh that's really sympathetic " huffed Gemma. It was true though, Ellie looked awful , she had dark shadows under her eyes and was as white as a sheet. She had also lost weight.

"You lost your phone remember" said Gemma for the hundredth time " he could be trying to get you and getting the lowlife who must have stolen your mobile."

" I know I thought of that, but the way that Gabriella spoke, he does it all the time."

" I am not so sure " frowned Gemma, "he seemed like a decent bloke. Why don't you ring Enzo and Maria at the hotel and ask them to pass on a message . Or try and get him at the ski school ? "

"I don't think so. I would feel really embarrassed . They would think I was just another silly girl."

" Well if you are sure" replied Gemma doubtfully.

Ellie had never felt so sad, she felt as if her whole world had ended. She couldn't be bothered to go out, except to work and she stayed at work to try and take her mind off things. She tried to cover it with a bright smile , but even her mum and dad had noticed. They arranged to take her to Mario's after work , to cheer her up, but Ellie didn't feel very hungry.

"Go on have a tiramisu love " coaxed her dad.

"No thanks I am really full and just need to pop to the toilet " and Ellie rushed to the toilet with tears streaming down her face. She stayed in the toilet until she had recovered. Hearing the waiters talking to each other in Italian had been hard , but the tiramisu had been the final straw. She had a vivid memory of Dario feeding her his grandmother's tiramisu.

"I think you should go to the doctor Ellie ." said her mum when she returned. "you haven't looked well since you came back from holiday."

"I am fine mum, stop fussing, it's such a depressing time of the year and most of the clients have colds. Shall we go now? Thank you for the meal it was lovely. " she smiled brightly at her parents. Once they dropped her at her flat she spent the evening playing music and crying .

A few weeks later Gemma went into the ladies to put on some lipstick before work and heard the sound of retching. Ellie came out of the toilet whiter than ever.

" Do you want to go home ? You look awful ."

" No it's O.K. I think I've got a bug, but I will feel better soon. I have been like it for the past few days but it always feels worse in the morning." Gemma stared at her and Ellie looked back in horror as the light began to dawn.

"Oh no I can't be "she breathed. " We were careful. Except the first time." she added.

"go and buy a pregnancy test . Now " ordered Gemma

Ellie's hand was shaking as she waited for the result, she felt dizzy and sick. The clear blue line showed that she was having Dario's baby. She put her head in her hands and sobbed.

" I can't I can't. How can I be pregnant ? Some people try for like years and years."

Gemma patted her back.

"Come on you don't have to have it. You go home for the rest of the day, take some time to think about your options."

Ellie couldn't remember the journey home. She got home, got into bed and then slept for a couple of hours. Then she rang Sam who came straight round. She put her arms around her while she sobbed. Ellie had told her all about Dario. He had sounded like the love of Ellie's life, she had never heard Ellie speak about anyone the way she had spoken about Dario. Sam knew that Ellie had been hoping that Dario would find a way of contacting her. When Ellie's sobs subsided Sam asked "what are you going to do about the baby?"

"keep it " replied Ellie shakily "it's a part of me and a part of Dario and I cannot destroy it"

"will you tell him?"

Ellie shook her head "if he cared he would have tried to contact me. He promised to see me before we left." she started to cry again. Sam hugged her, tears streaming down her face "I will help you. I will be the best aunty in the world . Do you want me to try and contact him, just once ? I think we should "

Elllie shook her head " Look at me . I am such a state. Who would want me now. Please just carry on being my friend but please, please don't try and contact him."

Ellie's parents were really supportive and suggested that she move back with them to save money. Ellie sold her share of her lovely little flat ,which she had worked hard to get and which she part owned, part rented from a housing association. She set up a nursery in the spare room at her parent's. Her parents tried to talk to her about Dario, but she just clammed up so they stopped asking. The pregnancy went really well apart from the sickness, although Ellie never really got her appetite back, but that was probably due to a broken heart. She felt really depressed and lethargic.Her hair was greasy, she had a horrible taste in her mouth and she had absolutely no energy. Her mum or Sam had attended all of the antenatal appointments with her. Sam was with her when she had a scan. What would she do if it was twins, she didn't feel ready to have one baby let alone two. She held her breath as the radiographer ran the machine across the gel on her stomach. She could see a few shapes , but couldn't make out what they were. The radiographer pointed out the head, body and arms and legs. It looked as if the baby was waving.

"well it looks like you are having a little boy " smiled the radiographer."

Ellie looked at the screen and burst into tears.

"hormones " smiled the radiographer.

" Come on let's go for a coffee and coo over the photo " said Sam linking her arm with Ellie's. "you will have to start thinking of boy's names now"

"I already have a boy's name." smiled Ellie and started to cry again.

It was strange, once she had had the scan and seen her baby on the screen it all became real. Ellie still felt panic when she thought about how she would cope but she was going to do her best for this little person. She had really loved his daddy, even if he did turn out to be a scumbag. She started eating healthily and exercising. The old Ellie started to return. She met some friendly mums to be at antenatal classes and went for a coffee with them afterwards. They agreed that they would all meet every few weeks once their babies were born. She was upset when she went to the antenatal classes and saw the doting fathers. Sam was great though and came to all of the classes, although there was some confusion at the first class when they introduced themselves and some people at the back thought Sam was a man. Ellie had picked up Sam one evening and was showing her photos of the baby's development in the book she had been given. Ralph looked over Sam's shoulder

"Eew that's disgusting " he said backing away.

'Ow ow!" Ellie had jumped out of bed quickly and her knee really hurt. She limped into work but could hardly stand up, she was clutching the desk.

" you need to go to A and E you can't be too careful when you are pregnant " exclaimed Gemma "come on I will drop you off "

At the hospital there were quite a few waiting . Ellie gave her details and limped to her seat. She was looking at her phone when she realised the nurse was calling her name. She hobbled in and the doctor looked at her over his glasses . Ellie carefully lowered herself onto the seat as she was getting quite big now.

"we need to do more tests , but it looks as though you might have to have two toes amputated if we can't sort you out."

Ellie looked in horror at her toes with the sparkly red nail varnish. She had been quite proud of them as she could hardly see her feet theses days. Her eyes filled with tears

"but it only started this morning when I jumped out of bed. I thought it was my knee. I didn't realise something like this could happen from being pregnant." and her mouth wobbled. The doctor looked confused

"you are Mary Holmes aren't you ? "

"no I am Ellie Stone."

Ellie realised she had not heard the nurse correctly. They were not very pleased with her and it didn't help that she kept looking at her toes and giggling while she was in the waiting area.

When she finally saw the doctor he informed her rather sternly that as she was pregnant her ligaments were softer and she had pulled something. She was told to rest her knee for a few days and she should see an improvement.

"Thank you ." muttered Ellie and escaped the hospital.

The nursery was almost completely furnished with the presents she had received from work, they had been so generous. Ralph and Mrs Brownridge were the only ones that had shown any disapproval. Sam had painted a beautiful farmyard mural on one wall of the nursery. The colourful farmyard animals were really cute and Ellie had made the whole room really bright with lightshades and stuffed toys. She had repainted an old chest of drawers and changed the knobs for some with animal heads that she had found.

Ellie was in her usual position being sick in the bathroom.

"I thought this was only supposed to last for three months " she said levering herself up from the toilet bowl.

"I was just the same with you and your brother" said Ellie's mom giving her a hug. " It will stop as soon as the baby is born. I will get you some more ginger biscuits. Your short hair looks really nice"

"No it doesn't but its easier when I'm being sick and when the baby comes there will be no hair to pull." Ellie sighed, Dario had loved her long hair. She felt that if she never saw another ginger biscuit it would be too soon. She hadn't missed having a drink as she didn't fancy one and the smell of coffee made her feel sick. One thing she had enjoyed was rocket ice lollies. The freezer was packed with them as she was eating around five each day.

They were brilliant at work and gave her a good send off and told her that she could come back to work once the baby was born. She had worked as long as she could so that she would have more time with the baby afterwards, although squeezing behind her desk was getting tricky , she had suddenly become the size of a hippopotamus.

Ellie heard a 'pop' and woke with a start. It was four in the morning and her waters had just broken. The baby wasn't due for another three weeks ! She phoned Sam who came straight round to take her to hospital. Ellie picked up her bag which was ready and waiting

"Don't forget I will come with you if you want "

Ellie's mum had been a bit put out when Ellie had chosen Sam as her birthing partner. Ellie thought her mum would stress her out with her yogic suggestions and she would get upset to see Ellie in pain.

" Here take this plant with you love. You can concentrate on it when you do your breathing. I read about it and I slipped some of that balm into your bag."

" Thanks mom " and Ellie gave her mom a big hug and then her dad.

Ellie put the plant down in the front garden when her mum was putting her bag into Sam's car and waved brightly to her dad who was standing in the doorway looking worried.

" I will be fine don't worry. Hopefully the next time I see you you will be grandparents."

Ellie felt suddenly frightened when she got into the car. This was it, there was no going back , she would be responsible for this small person until he became an adult. Also would it hurt much ?

"Just breathe deeply " Ellie muttered to herself and gripped the door of the car. She had put a towel on her seat as she didn't want to leave a puddle in Sam's car. Sam was driving faster than usual and looking a bit stressed. A strong contraction caught Ellie and she started panting.

"Please, please don't have the baby in the car. I don't know what to do. Keep your legs crossed "

"I'll try my best ." panted Ellie

The midwife who met them at the hospital was lovely and put her at ease, although she had now started to have fairly strong contractions at regular intervals. The labour was fairly short and after a few puffs of gas and air Sam started yelling that she could see a mass of dark hair and with one last push her son was born. Ellie held him in her arms with tears streaming down her face. Sam sat beside her blowing her nose noisily.

"He looks just like you"

"no he looks just like Dario" sobbed Ellie. " His hair kinks up on his forehead just like Dario's but don't tell anyone. They will think he looks like me." She gazed at her baby in amazement . How had she managed to produce this wonderful human being. She smiled and covered his little face with kisses. He had cried when he was born but was now sleeping peacefully.

" Here you can hold him"

Sam held him as if he was a bomb and gave him back after a few minutes as she was frightened of dropping him. They sat gazing at the baby in wonder .

"ooh let's see him" Ellie's mum burst into the room followed by her dad less than an hour later. They were both beaming.

"I might have known you wouldn't stay at home." sighed Ellie "come and meet your grandson."

"ooh the little darling he looks just like you. What are you calling him?"

"Alfie" said Ellie softly and she heard a strangled sob from Sam.

Ellie adored Alfie , she couldn't believe that she had produced this perfect little boy. She would sit holding him for hours, sometimes crying because his daddy couldn't see him and probably didn't care about him. Waves of overwhelming sadness engulfed her at times.

"never mind I promise to be the best mummy and you will never go without anything because you don't have a daddy." she whispered into his teeny tiny ear, as she wiped her tears off his head.

"It's baby blues " said her mum coming into the room. " come on wrap him up and we will go for a walk."

Her mum and dad had bought a gorgeous pushchair that she could change around as Alfie grew. They only walked down the road the first time but then she started walking around the village with him and felt better. Lots of people would peek into the pushchair and say what a gorgeous baby he was. Although he had been early he still had chubby little arms, legs and cheeks. She felt she had achieved something for them both to be dressed and out of the house, even if her shoulder always smelt of baby sick.

"He just smiled at me " she shrieked. Her mum came in wiping her hands on a tea towel
"they say it's wind but I am not convinced. I am sure he smiled at your dad last night."
Alfie was a happy contented baby, but he didn't sleep very well at night. He seemed to love people. He would lie contentedly in someone's arms and then the minute he was carefully lowered into his cot he would start to yell. Ellie would carefully carry him upstairs at snail pace and very gently lower him into his cot, taking one arm slowly from underneath him and then the other. Hardly daring to breathe she would slowly straighten up and then his eyes would shoot open and he would begin to howl. Sometimes she would lie by his crib stroking his head and then gradually lift her hand. She might even get to the door before he cried. Ellie couldn't believe the amount of work one little scrap could make. She seemed to be continually feeding, burping and changing him. In between she would be washing his clothes and sheets. He seemed to get through an awful lot of those. Ellie didn't manage to get dressed some days. She was so grateful that her parents were there, so that she could lie in the bath sometimes without worrying. He woke several times in the night and Ellie started giving him bottles in the hope he would sleep longer. She was so tired that she didn't think she was producing enough milk. Often she would find herself on the landing, not quite sure what she was doing there and one night her dad woke up to find Ellie with her arm under his head, trying to put a baby's bottle in his mouth.
"Er what are you doing?" he asked sleepily. Ellie jumped
"Oh sorry dad thought you were Alfie " she muttered and scuttled off to Alfie. After that it became a family joke, but her mum would look after Alfie one night a week to give Ellie some much needed rest. He was adored by everyone, even Sam's brother Andrew who was not at all keen on babies kept buying him teddies and toys.
"Take that out " ordered Ellie when Andrew walked in carrying a giant giraffe." If that goes in Alfie's room there won't be room for Alfie."

"Sorry " muttered Andrew sheepishly " I will swap it, do you think he would like a scalextric " he asked hopefully .

He loved lying on his mat and kicking his legs when his nappy was taken off and would gurgle delightedly when Sam blew raspberries on his stomach.

Sam adored him and was always finding excuses to pop in.

" It makes me want a baby" she sighed jiggling Alfie on her knee" but Ralph says we must get the house just right first. I am not that sure that he even likes babies."

" I wouldn't want him to be the father of any baby of mine" shuddered Ellie as she waved off Sam.

"no ' said her mum " he seems to be a very controlling sort of a person, a bit like Sam's mum."

Alfie would lie on his little mat, his little chubby arms waving madly at the toys above him. He would grab Ellie's finger and smile. When he was tired he would wind his fingers through Ellie's hair, she was pleased now that she had it cut shorter. She felt a tug at her heartstrings every time she looked at Alfie and felt sorry for Dario that he was missing out on this joy.

Eventually Ellie managed to get her and Alfie as far as the small town. nearby. One Wednesday morning Ellie's mum asked her to pay some money into the building society, when she was out shopping with Alfie. They had walked through the town and Ellie had bought herself some new trousers, Alfie had beamed at everyone, waving his little starfish hands, so she was feeling pleased with herself. They would just go into the building society and then go for a coffee.

" I am so sorry " said a scarlet faced Ellie to the cashier. Ellie had decided to pay the money into the credit point machine, but somehow she had posted it into the air vents at the side.

" I don't know what made me think that was the place." Ellie felt like crying, what had possessed her.

" Don't worry " said the cashier cheerfully " It's baby brain I was the same. I think we will have to call maintenance."

Ellie nodded glumly. If only she knew that these sort of disasters were common for Ellie. Later when Ellie was sitting in her favourite cafe nursing a latte she saw the funny side. She pictured the maintenance man's face as he fished out the notes. Her shoulders were shaking and she received a few strange looks.

" come on Alfie, let's go and tell grandma what your silly mummy did today."

Alfie grinned and waved his hands.

Ellie found that going out and about with Alfie she soon began to feel brighter. Alfie was a popular visitor at the estate agents.
"aw he's so cute." breathed Gemma lifting him out of his pushchair to give him a cuddle "come to your aunty Gemma " Alfie beamed and gurgled at Gemma.
"so" said Mark one day "when are you coming back to work?"
Ellie looked at Alfie's little face. How could she abandon this little baby. Gemma saw the look.
"Why don't you come back part time, say two and a half days a week? Say Mondays and Fridays when we are busy and half a day when you want. What do you think?" she looked at Mark
"That's fine by me, what do you say?"
"Oh that would be great" shrieked Ellie jumping up and down and hugging them both "Alfie is adorable but it would be lovely to have a conversation with an adult. I'm getting a bit sick of 'the wheels on the bus' ."
"poor little boy, has mummy been singing to you " cried Gemma cuddling Alfie "poor child won't recognise music if he has to listen to you." Ellie gave her a thump and rushed home to tell her mum. It was decided that his grandparents would look after him for one day and he would go to a childminder for one and a half days. It wasn't fair to ask her parents to have him more and anyway her mum had a part time job and her dad was working. His doting godmother Sam said she would babysit whenever she could so that Ellie could sometimes go out in the evenings.
"you should start an evening class or something and meet a nice man." Ellie wrinkled her nose at her " one step at a time. I will be lucky to get Alfie and I dressed and out of the house in time for work !"

Ellie felt as if she was slowly getting her life back but she wanted to be careful. She didn't want to leave Alfie with any old childminder. She saw often saw a childminder pass her mum's house. The child minder was sour faced and always looked grumpy. She would walk along pushing a pushchair with two children holding onto the handles, stopping every so often to look at her mobile. She didn't seem to interact with the children who were quite small . Later she would walk past with the addition of two school age children. The little ones were dragging their feet by this time and Ellie often felt like offering them a lift. Ellie trawled the internet . There was one which looked quite likely so Ellie left Alfie with her mum and dad and hid in the bushes outside the childminder's. She had checked that no one was looking before crouching down in her green jacket. There were two small children plonked in front of the television and two older boys were punching and kicking each other. Ellie wandered if she should go up to the house and intervene but the two smaller children were taking no notice and so it was probably a common occurrence. Then a woman came into the room and started shouting and screaming at the children. Ellie could hear her from her hiding place. She was hastily backing out of her hiding place when she noticed a dog walker advancing and pretended to fasten her shoelace , until she realised she was wearing boots, so she pulled a tissue out of her pocket and rubbed the toe of one boot.

"mud gets everywhere doesn't it ?" she muttered. The dog walker gave her a strange look and hurried on. Two other likely childminders had no vacancies and another had a dog that kept growling at Alfie when she went to visit.

"It's no good " said Ellie, she had rung Gemma to say she had had no luck with a childminder and so wouldn't be coming back to work at the moment.

" Let me ring my mum " replied Gemma "she said that her nice neighbour said that she wanted to take one child a few days a week , to help out with the bills. She has applied for all the permissions and checks. I will ring you back."

The neighbour said that she would like to meet Ellie.

"Will you come with me to see the child minder. I would like a second opinion and I am going to see her tonight, she sounds really nice. "

"course" replied Sam "what's her name?"

"Valentina"

"don't tell me, you picked her because she sounds Italian." said Sam rolling her eyes.

"come in come in" beamed Valentina .The house felt warm and cosy and there was the wonderful smell of garlic wafting from the kitchen. Valentina was tiny with rather shocking died red hair. She looked very chic. She had two children aged four and seven and she called them downstairs. They were two friendly imps with mops of unruly black curly hair. They started to push each other in a friendly way and rolled around the floor. Valentina started shouting to them in Italian and they ran upstairs giggling.

"now you will think I am a no good child minder" she cried

"no " said Ellie "this seems to be a happy house. So you are Italian? Valentina nodded

"yes me and my 'usband are from Rome. 'e works long hours in a restaurant. I love children but it is not possible for me to 'ave more."

Ellie glanced at Sam who nodded and smiled at her.

"I would like you to be Alfie's child minder if you agree. "

Valentina beamed and gave her a hug. " good, good 'e is a lovely little boy ' and she pinched Alfie's cheeks . Alfie giggled and pointed at the two children who had crept back downstairs . They had brought some of their toys to show Alfie. Their mother gabbled to them in Italian and appeared to have told them that they would be looking after Alfie. They both jumped up and down and gave Alfie a smacking kiss. Alfie gurgled with pleasure.

"Alfie you are going to come to our house and we will play with you."

Alfie blew a raspberry , which the children thought was hysterical. Ellie smiled and turned to Valentina

" Could I ask you one thing?"

Valentina looked at her enquiringly.

"could you speak to him in Italian when he is with you. His daddy is Italian but he isn't with us "

Valentina beamed and patted Ellie's hand

"of course. It will be a pleasure and I will cook for the bambino good Italian food ."

" you have found a good one there " said Sam. Ellie nodded happily.

Now she could go back to work and hopefully her work clothes would still fit.

CHAPTER NINE

Alfie settled in well at Valentina's and he loved the two children . He would follow them adoringly as soon as he was able to toddle. They involved him in their games and Ellie often arrived to find him sitting chuckling in the trailer while they rode around in a tractor pretending he was a little pig. Best of all was listening to him chattering in Italian as he got older. He had even learnt some Italian nursery rhymes .

" Look how beautiful Alfie looks." said Domenica one day pulling Ellie into the room. She had covered Alfie's face with her mum's lipstick and eyeshadow. He had two big red circles on his cheeks, clown like lips and blue eyeshadow on his forehead. He beamed at Ellie. Valentina came into the room and screamed

" What have you done to Alfie. The poor bambino. You are naughty girl and you use my make up. You say sorry to Alfie and his mummy now."

Domenica burst into tears

"I'm sorry Ellie I was just making Alfie pretty. Sorry Alfie." and she hugged Alfie. Alfie beamed at her and held his arms out to be picked up. He didn't care that he looked like something out of a horror film. Ellie found it difficult to keep a straight face

"That's OK Domenica but maybe don't do it again, or use mummy's make up without asking her. I'll go and get some tissues to clean his face." and she dashed into the kitchen before the children could see her laughing. Valentina joined her and she started laughing. It was a while before they could go back i with the tissues.

"Don't let her near any scissors will you. One of our clients came in with her children and the little girl had a fringe so short it was sticking up in the air. her fringe wasn't long enough to tie back so her older sister kindly cut it for her."

Ellie had gained some of the weight she had lost from being so sick during pregnancy and her face no longer looked gaunt. The weight she had gained had only been around her bump and that soon disappeared. She still had a flabby tummy but was doing some yoga with her mum and was starting to see the benefit. This didn't stop Valentina from trying to fatten her up. She was always leaving with Alfie and a container of food.

"you were too skinny, but now you looking much better." beamed Valentina

"If you carry on giving me all this food I will have to buy bigger clothes !" replied Ellie hoisting Alfie up on one arm and what looked like some sort of fruit cake in the other. Alfie waved goodbye to Valentina and blew her kisses. She had started having a private Italian lesson with Valentina once a week, which she really enjoyed. Valentina asked them to dinner about once a month. She had a rule that they must only speak in Italian during the meal. Alfie would sit in his high chair banging a spoon. Ellie loved it, it was like being part of a big noisy family, the only problem was the never ending food. After the first meal Ellie staggered to the car with Alfie , she was so stuffed she could hardly move.

" Ellie, Ellie you take this for your mama and papa " and Valentina would press more food on her. The problem was it was all so delicious that Ellie couldn't resist it.

Work was going well. It was the best of both worlds, she had adult company and enjoyed a laugh at work but still had time to go out and about with Alfie. They walked miles with the pushchair and visited lots of playgrounds and soft play places. They also met some of the antenatal mums and their babies. It was good as they could share their problems and tips. Who would have thought that she could discuss teething for twenty minutes she thought, smiling at the tired faces of the other mums. Ellie sometimes cried quietly at night when she sat by Alfie when he was fast asleep, his long dark lashes fanning his face.

"Oh you are so like your daddy " she would whisper. She wondered if Dario was still playing the field, or if he had settled down and got married.

"I couldn't bear it if he has had another child." she thought

Alfie had a nasty cough and Ellie took him to the doctors before she went to work. After a few sleepless nights she was feeling shattered. It was a chest infection and the doctor gave Alfie a prescription for antibiotics. Alfie was unusually clingy and she felt guilty leaving him with her mum while she went to work.

" Don't worry " said her mom " we are going to snuggle up on the sofa and watch Peppa Pig, aren't we Alfie."

Alfie pulled the dummy out of his mouth, coughed and nodded and then popped the dummy back.

" I am just nipping to the chemist with Alfie's prescription " she shouted at lunchtime " does anyone want anything.

" Oh could you drop that five hundred pound deposit at the bank please. Mrs Davies insisted that we have a deposit to show that she is keen, even though I told her it wasn't necessary." Gemma handed Ellie the credit point envelope to post in the bank.

" I am sure it was in my bag" Ellie hurriedly scrabbled in her bag for Alfie's prescription. She pulled out her purse, dummies, coins, a toy bear, lipstick brush, fork, screwdriver. In the end she emptied her bag on the floor, but couldn't find his prescription anywhere.
" Sorry I will have to come back later "
The pharmacy assistant assured her that they were open late. Ellie trudged back to work, she would have to call in the doctors again and ask if they could let her have another prescription. Later in the afternoon Mark received a phone call from the bank. He strolled over and sat on Ellie's desk with a grin on his face.
" well we know what happened to Alfie's prescription , you posted it in the bank with the envelope !"
" Noo !" Ellie buried her head in her hands.
" Go on, go to the bank and call in the chemists and get Alfie's medicine while you are at it. What is it with you and posting stuff ! I thought it was the little kids you had to watch ."

Alfie recovered from his chest infection and Ellie caught up with some sleep. She decided that she should start going out a bit more into the outside world and maybe find a man. It would be good to have someone to share the evenings with once Alfie had gone to bed. She often went to her room to watch tv, as her mum and dad didn't share her taste in tv programmes and she wanted to give them space. She went for a drink after work a few times , but didn't meet anyone although it was good to catch up with the crowd. Gemma and Mark were now engaged and making wedding plans, but Kate and Will had split up. Mel and Max had moved in together. Mel would always ask to see the latest Alfie photos and check that Ellie was doing O.K. She even offered to babysit, but Ellie felt that she didn't know her well enough to ask and anyway where would she go ? Sam would come over at least once a week and they would have a takeaway or go for a meal if Ellie's mum and dad babysat. "Well we are here anyway, you go and have some fun" they would say. Ellie didn't want to put on them too much, Alfie's toys were scattered all over the place. Besides money was tight as she was trying to save for a deposit on their own place, to add to the share of her flat sale that was in the bank. Her mum and dad loved him to bits , but she knew they needed their own space. She was worried about how Alfie would get on without a garden, as it was unlikely that they would be able to afford a house. He loved playing outside and helping grandad.

"I will have to find a nice man " she told herself "not some Italian Romeo."

Sam suggested a dating agency and Ellie reluctantly decided to give Tinder a go. " make sure you meet in a public place" warned Sam. She had helped Ellie with the profile photo. Ellie's hair was growing back and the photo looked good but not fake. Ellie refused to pout and said she wanted to find someone who liked natural women as she didn't have the time or inclination for botoxed lips and heavy eyebrows. She would struggle to shave her legs and put on nail varnish for a date.

Ellie read Adam's profile again, he liked music and going to the cinema and looked nice enough and he had swiped her. She didn't want too much excitement and decided to give it a go after discussing it with Sam. She arranged to meet him at the cinema. Ellie pulled into the car park, bits of mud were dropping off the mini as she had been showing a farmhouse earlier in the day. The inside of her car was a mess, she really needed to give it a good clean. Whilst she was scrabbling around for her bag a car parked in the bay in front of her and the man who got out looked suspiciously like Adam's photo. Ellie sank down into the seat and watched. He opened the boot and took out a steering wheel lock. Who knew that people still used those? He then spent a good ten minutes checking the locks and windows and walking around the car. He glanced at the mini and tutted and shook his head,

"eek I can't face this" decided Ellie and fastened her seatbelt ready to leave, but she was too kind hearted, so she waited for Adam to walk into the cinema and followed.

"Hi " she tapped Adam on the shoulder. He turned around and beamed at her. He insisted on paying and they sat down.

"oh he's quite sweet" thought Ellie and then gulped as he took off his coat to reveal the same jumper as the one her mum bought her dad last Christmas.

They went for a drink after the film and Adam went on and on about the director, producer, and cast. It seemed he was quite a film buff. Ellie felt herself drifting off and was embarrassed when Adam nudged her awake. She must have nodded off, how awful.

"Oh sorry " gabbled Ellie, wiping the dribble off the corner of her mouth "it's been a long day I really must be going. Thank you for a lovely evening"

She reported to Sam

" I am sorry he was a nice, kind man, but not for me. I feel awful , he messaged me and I pretended I had got back with an old boyfriend. It feels so cruel."

Then there was Nigel of the little purse. They went for a meal . He took ages choosing from the menu, he asked her if she wanted wine and she refused as she was driving. He offered coffee later and sounded as though he was going to treat her. Ellie would have refused as she always offered to pay her way, but at the end of the meal he carefully totted up Ellie's share, frowning as the figures didn't add up, face clearing as he realised it was Ellie's extra mushrooms, which he quickly added to her bill.

Dan seemed to be lovely and they had a few dates. Afterwards Ellie thought that maybe he just seemed lovely in comparison to the other dates. Ellie always told her dates in advance about Alfie as they came as a package They had got on so well that after two dates Ellie suggested that they all went to the park together. Dan kept trying to kiss her when Alfie was about, but the final straw was when Alfie ran over to her with a daisy he had picked and Dan said in an irritated voice "just go and play over there for a bit son and give your mum and I a bit of peace."
Alfie gazed up at Dan with a frown on his little face.
"he is NOT your son and he is not going over there" stormed a horrified Ellie
"Come on Alfie let's go and have a piece of cake and watch Peppa Pig " and taking Alfie's hand she stalked off. On the way home Alfie had been quiet and then he said
" mummy, Domenica and Stefano have a daddy, why don't I have one?"
Ellie bent down and hugged Alfie. She explained that he did have a daddy who lived in another country and spoke Italian like Valentina.
"why can't I see my daddy?" asked Alfie screwing up his face
"because your daddy has to work in the other country. The country is called Italy. It's a long way away and he has to work very hard ."explained Ellie.
"will I see him one day?"
"I expect so" replied Ellie with a lump in her throat.
That night Ellie cried herself to sleep, something she had not done since Alfie was very small. Sometimes she wondered if she should try and get in touch with Dario for Alfie's sake , but she was pretty sure that he wouldn't want to know and so wouldn't that rejection be far worse for Alfie ?

She couldn't bear to see Alfie upset, the way he had been today. Anyway it was a bit late now Alfie was two and getting bigger every day.

Alfie was adorable and if it was going to be just the two of them that was fine. He was funny and mischievous and they had a great time together. He would twinkle at her with Dario's eyes and her heart would melt.

"mummy, mummy let's go to the park" he would beg, smothering her face with wet kisses.

She tried really hard not to spoil him and refused to let him have sweets every time they went into a shop. To give him his due he never asked and often took his sweets to share with Stefano and Domenica. Her parents indulged Alfie's every whim and she was constantly telling them that they mustn't spoil him as she didn't want a spoilt brat on her hands. He occasionally had a terrible twos tantrum, but on the whole he was very well behaved. He always said 'please' and 'thank you' and was very kind.

He had a meltdown one day when he wanted to climb into the car and car seat himself. He had been messing around so Ellie had lifted him in. Alfie promptly got out and then in again by himself. He then wanted to fasten the straps on his seat, but couldn't quite manage it. He was getting more and more frustrated but wouldn't let Ellie do it.

" Come on Alfie let mummy do it or I will be late for work."

"No" shouted Alfie throwing his shoe across the car. Ellie sighed

"How about if I hold the strap this side and you plug it in."

"No I do it." Ellie sat there for a further five minutes while Alfie got more and more frustrated.

"Look Alfie" she said gently children's car seats are for grown ups to fasten, so they can check that their children are nice and safe. Will you let me try ?"

"If you want but I don't like you any more." he screamed and threw his other shoe across the car. He then cried all the way to Valentina"s and refused to kiss her goodbye."

"Is the terrible twos " said Valentina "just keep calm, they frustrated when they can't do stuff."

"Deep breathing and roll on third birthday then" said Ellie as she drove off. By the time she picked him up Alfie was back to his usual sunny self smothering her in kisses.

Ellie drove home after a trying day at work, a client was insisting that the kitchen in his new home was different from the kitchen he had been shown when he viewed the property. The photo of the kitchen on the website was not very clear as it had mostly shown the breakfast bar and dining area. How was she supposed to deal with that allegation? She could hear Alfie shouting

"mummy mummy I have been digging look"

Ellie looked at her dad puzzled. He shrugged

"I don't know what he is talking about.....unless oh my seeds" and her dad dashed off to the conservatory where Alfie was brandishing a fly swatter covered in mud and several plant pots were on their side.

"Oh Alfie that's naughty you have tipped out all of Grandad's seeds that he planted the other day"

"Sorry grandad I was helping" said Alfie a large tear rolling down his face. He hugged his grandad who promptly melted

"never mind you didn't know, come and help me plant them again and then you must leave them alone."

Alfie nodded solemnly and followed his grandad.

"we really must find somewhere to live and give mum and dad some peace' thought Ellie and then her mobile rang

"Hi Sam........what's the matter?"

"Ellie please come over......it's mum she has died" sobbed Sam

Ellie jumped into her car and rushed over to Sam's. She was in quite a state when Ellie got there, apparently her mother had been yelling at some teenagers who were sitting on her wall chatting outside her house, when she had had some sort of a seizure and dropped down dead. The shocked kids had telephoned for an ambulance, but it was too late. They said that they thought she had died instantly. The police had called at Sam's house to tell her. Ralph had been in an important meeting when Sam rang him and said he could not leave, the pig.

Ellie comforted Sam and went with her to the mortuary, which was awful poor Sam couldn't stop sobbing.

" It's the shock" said Ellie " It was so sudden. It's not as if she had been ill."

" No, I have never known mum be ill . I never had a chance to say goodbye. We weren't as close as you and your mum but she was my mum." and she started crying again.

Ellie took her back home and was just making Sam some soup when Ralph walked in.

"I'm so sorry darling what a terrible thing to happen." he said hugging her.

"do you want me to do anything?" Sam clung to him crying and he patted her back gingerly

"no it's OK Ellie is coming with me tomorrow to get the death certificate and go to the undertakers" she sobbed

"well if you are sure" he said with relief " I do have another meeting with those important clients tomorrow and it wouldn't look good if I cancel. I don't want to spoil those partnership prospects. Let me make you a nice cup of tea."

When he came back from the kitchen he said

"I can help sort out the financial stuff for your mother's estate and with the house sale. That house must be worth a fair bit now."

Ellie was appalled, she hadn't liked Mrs Brownridge much , but the poor woman was hardly cold. Hers eyes met Sam's but neither of them said anything.

The next day Ellie left Alfie with her parents, then she helped with all of the arrangements and she rang around Mrs Brownridge's family and friends. Sam's dad came over as soon as he heard and sat hugging Sam for a long time.

"You can come over to my house now whenever you like, both kids are away at the moment ,one is working away, the other is at university but they would love to meet you when they get back. They have always thought of you as family you know and Pat would love to meet you again. We would be happy for you to stay with us."

"Thanks Dad" sniffed Sam.

" I mean it, I haven't seen enough of you growing up and I want to see a lot more of you now. Ring me if you need anything at all. Pat made a casserole for you and Ralph. I'll just get it from the car " He stopped and frowned " but where is Ralph ? "

" Oh he had to go to work, for an important meeting."

Mr Brownridge frowned at Ellie over Sam's head and Ellie shrugged in reply.

The funeral took place on a beautiful April morning at their lovely village church. It didn't seem five minutes since Sam was walking down the isle to marry Ralph. Ellie was pleased for Sam that there was quite a good turnout, with the bridge, choir and golf club members. Ellie's mum and dad

attended and Alfie was at Valentina's. After the service Sam was chatting to people and then she went to look at the flowers. She heard one old lady ask her friend
"How is your Bert?"
"Oh he is is fine "replied the other. " Grumpy as ever. He is 97 now you know. Whoever would have thought that he would live that long! " and then she sighed deeply and walked away. Sam looked over at Ralph busy socialising with the golf crowd . He was laughing at something someone said and was in his element. He had not comforted Sam and had walked around her mum's house picking up various items to see if they were worth anything when they were awaiting the funeral cars. She thought "I can't do this any more. I don't love him, I don't think I ever have and it has got to stop. I can't do this for another sixty years." then she smiled tearfully at Ellie who was watching her anxiously .

At the wake she stopped to chat with Sam's mum's neighbour Joyce, who had always been very kind to Sam and had volunteered at the same charity shop that Mrs Brownridge had worked at.
" Sam is a lovely girl." said Joyce sipping her sherry " but truth be told I never got on with her mum, always moaning about something she was, but I mustn't speak ill of the dead."
" I think that there are quite a few people here who think the same way . " smiled Ellie. It was a shame as Sam appeared to be the only person who was genuinely upset.
" Here have this drink" Ellie passed Sam a large glass of wine and made her sit down. " This has all been very stressful for you. You must look after yourself. Do you want me to stay at your's tonight ? "
Sam shook her head " I will be fine thanks Ellie and thanks for everything." Sam looked pale but something looked different about her.

CHAPTER TEN

" You have done what" exclaimed Ellie, her eyes as round as saucers

"I have moved into mum's house and am divorcing Ralph" smiled Sam and she really smiled , like the old Sam.

"Wow when did this happen?"

"Well I decided at the funeral, but it took two weeks for me to pluck up courage and I had to make plans. Anyway on Tuesday Ralph came home from work in a foul mood and criticised the cleanliness of the house and said his dinner was inedible, although he managed to eat most of it. So I suggested he cook it himself in future as I was leaving and I picked up my bag and walked out of the door. I said that I would be back for my stuff and to sort out the arrangements for him buying me out of the house. You should have seen his face! Will you come with me to collect my stuff ? Oh Ellie I feel that such a weight has been lifted."

"Course I will " said Ellie hugging her so tightly that she squeaked. " How did Ralph take it ?"

" Well I think he was more annoyed at losing a personal housekeeper and how it would look with his work colleagues. I don't think he was exactly heartbroken."

" You have done the right thing and now you can start living the life you want."

Sam nodded

" I had been thinking about it just before mum died, I realised I was doing less and less of the things I liked and was always walking on eggshells, but I became absolutely certain at the funeral. I knew that it would make mum happy to see me married to Ralph, but I shouldn't have let myself be persuaded. Life is too short and she shouldn't really have asked it of me. I miss her but it feels odd that there is no one criticising me any more. I feel sort of free. Dad's been great and visiting his happy home made me realise that that is what I want someday. Now, where's my favourite boy?"

"Here I am aunty Sam" said Alfie, who had taken advantage of the drama . He was sitting under the table and had eaten a chocolate biscuit, or maybe two from the state of his face.

He gave Sam a big chocolatey kiss and then hugged her because he said that he knew she was sad because of her mummy.

Sam blinked back the tears and gave Alfie a big hug. "Thank you Alfie, do you know that you always give the best hugs ? "

Alfie nodded solemnly and then said "Can Aunty Sam stay for dinner? Look she has a tiramisu in her bag."

" I suppose so, but how do you know that the tiramisu is for us? Aunty Sam might be taking it home."

Alfie looked worried and then beamed when Sam took the tiramisu out of her bag and put it on the table.

Ellie smiled, Alfie also loved tiramisu and loved going for lunch with mummy and Aunty Sam. Needless to say Aunty Sam spoiled him rotten. He might not have a daddy but he was surrounded by love, which was a million times better than having a daddy like Ralph. He joined in with marking the tiramisu but always gave it 'a hundred million'. He got that from Stefano.

"mummy have you ever had a number ten tiramisu?" he asked later licking his spoon.

"Once when I was with your daddy. His grandma made one which was a ten."

"Oh, can I have some more please? "

Ellie glanced at Sam who shrugged. She would try and answer Alfie's questions as and when they arose, but tiramisu was obviously priority at the moment.

" Mine too " muttered Ellie helping herself to more.

Over the next few weeks Sam saw a solicitor and sorted out her mum's estate and instructed a divorce lawyer. It looked as though Ralph would do fairly well out of it, due to her mum's death, but the solicitor thought he would be able to do a deal so that Sam cut all ties with him and had no claim on his pension etc. Ralph had always been secretive about money and Ellie thought he probably had some hidden away.

" There will be enough money to buy my own little place, with enough leftover to keep me going if I get short of commissions " she told Ellie. "No mortgage, no pressures, I am so lucky. I would love a little cottage with a garden. I want to get into gardening and it's always useful to have some flowers to copy for my illustrations. "

Sam had gained in confidence over the last couple of weeks and was busy making all sorts of plans.

" Brilliant you can join me internet dating ! Too soon ? " she grinned looking at Sam's horrified face.

CHAPTER ELEVEN

Ellie looked up from her desk to see a tall man with mad brown curly hair grinning at her
"Hi could you help me please. I need someone to help me sell my great aunt's house, as she has gone into a nursing home. My name is Xander, by the way."
"wow" thought Ellie " he is nice .
" I am sure we can help, now let's take down some details " she said grabbing a pen and trying to ignore Gemma's thumbs up signals from the back of the office.

Gemma suggested to Mark, with much winking at Ellie, that Ellie should go on the viewing with Mark.
"he is just your type "she hissed "and he has a lovely smile."
"He certainly has " thought Ellie " come on girl go for it."
Xander chatted to Ellie as Mark was writing down measurements . He seemed really friendly. He lived locally and had been helping to take care of his aunt. Ellie tried flirting a little, although she was still not very good at it and stopped flicking her hair after she caught Xander in the face and he looked a bit alarmed.

The next time Ellie went into work Gemma grabbed her.
"Xander rang and asked to speak to you. I told him that you weren't at work and he made up some excuse as to why he called."
Later that morning Xander rang again .
" Hi do you fancy going out for a drink on Friday night ? There's a band playing at my local."
"That would be great. I will just have to check that I can get a babysitter."
" Fine just give me a ring and let me know."
Ellie wasn't sure if she was supposed to date clients, or relatives of clients and she wasn't about to ask.
"Well Gemma demanded was that him ?"
"yes and I mentioned that I would need a babysitter and he didn't seem fazed that I had a child. It looks as though I am going on a date. Woohoo !"

Ellie changed her clothes three times before she left for the date. In the end she put on her jeans and a pretty flowery top. She didn't want to seem too anxious. The date was a great success and as a band was playing she didn't feel the need to make conversation all night. When Xander smiled he had a lovely little dimple in one cheek and for the first time in a long time Ellie felt the first stirrings of lust. He kissed her passionately at the end of the night and they arranged to go for a meal the following week. Xander asked about Alfie and seemed genuinely interested. They chatted all through the meal, they liked music, although their taste was not quite the same. Xander seemed to have a good knowledge of up and coming bands that Ellie had never even heard of.

" I can see I will have to educate you " he said and then told her all about his travels. He had been all over the world. He explained that he had been engaged four years before, but had not got travelling out of his system and they split up.

" I still like travelling but I think am ready to settle down now. At least that is what my mum keeps telling me. " he smiled.

Ellie felt a lurch of panic at the thought of settling down with anyone, but decided he was just explaining that he would not be off on his travels any time soon and anyway she couldn't see Xander making that type of decision any time soon. They agreed to meet a few days later.

Xander was very easy going , to say he was laid back was an understatement. He was virtually horizontal and nothing stressed him. She really liked him and could be herself , she didn't feel the need to dress up and impress him. He met Ellie after work and they went to The Red Lion for a quick drink.

" I am so happy that I chose your estate agents. "

" I bet you are now that I have agreed to help you clear your aunties house. " she retorted.

Xander wasn't even bothered by Ron who had studiously ignored him at the bar several times. Xander had simply waited and chatted to whoever was propping up the bar. Ellie didn't think he had even noticed. She went back to Xander's flat that night. It was lovely to be with someone again, although there were no fireworks.

" I just need to be realistic " she thought. after all she wasn't ever likely to meet another Dario.

" Who wants to go to the safari park? " asked Xander when he rang two nights later. "I have discount vouchers and you could bring Alfie. I would like to meet him. Unless you think it is too early" he added anxiously.

" No that would be fine. Thank you. Alfie will adore the safari park.

Alfie was running around placing things in his dinosaur back pack.
" You won't need felt pens and your toy reindeer at the safari park ! " exclaimed Ellie , removing the items.
"here put in this jumper and your drink bottle. I think I can hear Xander outside."
Ellie's dad welcomed Xander into the house and he chatted to her mum and dad for a few minutes and then knelt down in front of Alfie.
" Hi you must be Alfie. I have heard that you like animals, so we should see quite a few today, but not dinosaurs " he smiled glancing at the back pack.
" Will they have a hippopotamus do you think." asked Alfie " I like hippotamuses and I know a lot about them " he added proudly.
" I think maybe they do." said Xander nodding seriously.

They had a wonderful day . Xander had listened patiently to Alfie's chatter about the various animals, they had a picnic and Xander made Alfie laugh when he pretended to accidentally sit on his sandwich." you have a lovely little boy " said Xander as they watched Alfie on the roundabout. Then he ran around the roundabout pretending to try and catch Alfie which Alfie thought was hilarious.
" I think I need to sit down " said Xander when Ellie went to collect Alfie " I have gone a bit dizzy."
Xander was like a big kid himself and was enthusiastic about everything. He insisted on going on all the rides that he could. She had to drag them both off the ride that fired lasers.
" I don't think you will fit in that zebra Xander " said Alfie critically as he watched Xander trying to squish himself into a ride. Ellie had to help pull him out, which took a while as they were all laughing so much.

Alfie came home bursting with excitement . He told his grandparents about all the animals he had seen and showed them the toy penguin that Xander had brought him.
" I wanted to hold a penguin but you are not allowed you know. I think I am going to be a zookeeper when I grow up. Then I could hold the penguins."

Ellie and Xander became more serious and he met Sam and they went for a drink with Ellie's friends from work and she met Xander's friends who were lovely. Sam and the others thought he was great. He was really sporty and made Ellie feel tired as he was always going off for a game of tennis or football. In fact he tried to pack too much into the day sometimes , which made him late, but he would just shrug and grin. He didn't even bother wearing a watch. If he met someone who wanted a game of football , he would just go and then probably stay chatting for ages and lose all track of time.

" hey don't stress just let's enjoy ourselves " was a common response.

He patiently kicked a ball around the garden for Alfie who kept shouting

" kick it to me again "cus I am going to get another goal"

" Oh no not another" said Xander in mock despair, which made Alfie giggle.

" It's lovely to see Alfie playing with Xander smiled her mum. You have got a good one there."

Ellie agreed that it was, it felt like they were a proper little family, although they should have picked up Sam half an hour ago.

Ellie stayed at Xander's flat once a week and felt really comfortable there. She did not feel a whirling sensation when Xander kissed her but you couldn't have everything. He was so thoughtful and kind. He had lately taken an interest in the houses that Ellie's estate agents were selling and making comments such as " That one has a lovely long garden, you could put some football goals in there."

This was all a bit scary, but Ellie allowed herself to dream of how much easier her and Alfie's futures would be if they all lived together in a house. She would love a big garden with a swing and a slide for Alfie. Still she wouldn't have to think about that for ages as it would take forever for Xander to do something about buying a house.

CHAPTER TWELVE

Sam was living at her mum's house, although there was now a 'for sale ' board in the front garden. Ellie called at the house and sniffed a familiar smell.

"You are painting again!"

"Yes" beamed Sam, there is loads of room here and I keep losing track of time and painting 'till the early hours, although I will have to do a quick tidy if someone comes to view."

"That's why I called. There are three viewings arranged for Friday."

"That's brilliant, there is a lovely little cottage I saw advertised last week. Fingers crossed that someone out there likes lots of chintz. I have taken down all the lace curtains and thrown away the lace toilet dollies. I have also hidden all the china figurines and cut glass. Who knew she had one hundred and twelve figurines ! "

" Have you heard from Ralph ?"

" No but I received a letter from my solicitor setting out my options and saying that his solicitor has been in touch, so it's looking hopeful.

Sam took Ellie upstairs to see the huge painting that she was working on. It was a beautiful view of the Cotswolds with a golden setting sun. She had a similar smaller one packed away from her flat. Sam had given it to her on her twenty first birthday. One day she would be able to unpack it again.

"you really are good you know. You should have your own exhibition. "

"Thanks " Sam started fiddling with her paintbrushes "Umm by the way have you heard that Rick's band have become quite successful and are touring the U.K.?"

"No !" exclaimed Ellie. " I hadn't heard but we only seem to have nursery rhymes on in the car and Peppa Pig on the tv these days."

Sam was looking very bright eyed and bushy tailed.

"Were you thinking of going to one of the gigs?"

"well it wouldn't harm would it. Actually I messaged his facebook page last week and he is arranging for us to have free tickets at the front . You will come with me won't you ? "

"Oh right, yes of course I will. It will be good to get out and hear how he is getting on. Do you think you still have feelings for him? "

"I don't think so " shrugged Sam , "but it would be lovely to catch up and I think I am due a bit of fun."

"You certainly do " agreed Ellie " fun here we come. Now how about we put out a couple of vases of flowers and could you take that hideous picture down and replace it with one of yours ?"

A few days later Sam called into Ellie's to see if there was any news regarding her sale
" No but I am sure that second couple are going to make an offer. I am trying to scare them into hurrying up as I have implied that there is someone else interested."
"You look a bit worried. Are you OK " frowned Sam.
"yes I am fine " replied Ellie " but it's Xander…."
" I thought you two were an item now. He hasn't done anything to upset you has he? "
" No the opposite if anything. He is so kind and caring and I fancy him but .."
" He is not Dario " finished Sam
" No, but well I don't think it's that, but he seems to be getting serious very quickly, which isn't really like him. He keeps asking what sort of houses I like, as he is going to sell his flat and buy a house. I am sure he is going to ask me to move in with him. I have already met his mum and dad . I don't know if it's because he is really keen on me or he has just decided to become an adult. I keep thinking how good it would be for Alfie, he adores Xander and it would solve all our problems. I feel horrible because he is absolutely lovely but I don't love him. I have really, really tried. I am a horrible person aren't I ? "
" No of course you are not, but I think you need to tell him, it's not fair on him is it ? "
" No " agreed Ellie " I think I have been kidding myself as it has been lovely being part of a couple and Alfie really likes him. You are right though it's not fair on him."
" Please don't make the same mistake as me." said Sam hugging her " Let me know how you get on."

Sam agreed to sell the house at a good price and her offer was accepted on a lovely little cottage at the edge of the village which was pure Sam with an inglenook fireplace and country kitchen. There were even roses around the door. She couldn't wait to move in but the conveyancing was dragging, someone at the top if the chain was having problems with a survey. It felt strange living in her mum's house and she couldn't wait to put her stamp on the cottage. Ralph had made most of the decisions regarding furnishing her old house.

"I am so glad that you are my agent and can keep reassuring me." said Sam, arriving at Ellie's with an armful of toys for Alfie, a lemon drizzle cake and a dvd. "Never mind it's Miasma's concert next week."

" yes it will be good to see Rick again and don't worry I don't think there will be any problems with the chain. "

"Actually Rick's messaged me a few times. He has asked me to go out for a meal after the concert." blushed Sam.

"oh right..um that's good , only don't build up your hopes and you have only just come out of a relationship remember."

"I know, I know but I just want to have some fun like we used to. You know"

"Yes " smiled Ellie, " those days seem a long time ago " and she burst into tears.

" Oh no" what's the matter cried Sam hugging Ellie.

Ellie sobbed for a while before she could speak.

" I, I finished with Xander last night " hiccuped Ellie " he was really upset and I felt like the worst person in the world. He sent me a lovely text this morning. He is going to make someone a wonderful husband , just not me. Alfie asked me this morning when we were going to see Xander again and burst into tears when I said I wasn't Xander's friend anymore. I think Alfie hates me now, I have had some very stroppy looks and he said that Xander was still his friend. Have I done the right thing ? We could have had a lovely life and Alfie would have had the best step dad. "

" You did the right thing" sighed Sam

" so we are both young , free and single again, although not quite as young as we were." sniffed Ellie wiping the mascara off her cheek.

Sam changed her outfit three times while Ellie patiently waited.

"Do you think this looks OK? ' She twirled around showing black skinny jeans and a dark green floaty top

"Isn't that the one you wore first?"

"Yes but I have changed my boots."

"It's fine come on! Remember you are not that bothered"

Sam smiled and nodded and then went back to the mirror to check her hair. Ellie rolled her eyes, it looked like there could be trouble ahead.

The concert was not in a large stadium but it was a decent sized venue and was a sell out.
Rick was very charismatic on stage and Ellie felt proud that they knew him. Sam was very starry eyed. Ellie felt swept away and was dancing and singing with the rest of the crowd. They were both amazed that the crowd knew the words to the songs. As it was the home crowd the atmosphere was even better.

"Wow " exclaimed Sam " to think that that last song was written when we were sitting in your mum's garden."

Ellie nodded she couldn't believe that they knew an actual rock star. After the concert security lead them to the backstage area and Rick's dressing room. He was bawling at some poor man.

"I said I wanted peanut butter sandwiches and white tulips in my dressing room NOT white roses."

Ellie snorted with amusement and then realised that everyone was deadly serious. The poor man was explaining how hard it was to obtain tulips in June. Rick suddenly spotted them.

"Hi babes great to see you" and he air kissed both of them. "Come on in. Hey folks Sam here was my first love and I have never really forgotten her " Sam blushed as he blew her kisses "We'll get out of here, you coming Ellie?"

Ellie had planned on leaving Sam but her friend looked like a startled deer caught in the headlights, so she said she would go with them for a while. They went back to Rick's hotel where food and drink was brought in for the entourage. Rick clicked his fingers rather a lot and sat with his arm draped around Sam while Ellie chatted to the band and roadies. The drink was flowing and Ellie had helped herself to several. Rick still looked handsome, but he seemed thinner and there were shadows under his eyes. There was also quite a lot of white powder scattered on the tables.

"So you used to go to school with Rick?" asked Ed one of the roadies.

Ellie nodded

"Poor you. I'm off next week I have a job lined up with another band"

"but he used to be good fun, he was always making us laugh" frowned Ellie.

"well he must have lost it because he is a nightmare now. He has also started turning up late on stage. He does it deliberately . I have worked for people like him in the past and I am not putting up with it. Do you fancy a drink in the hotel bar ?"

Ellie glanced at Sam who now relaxed and laughing at something Rick said and mouthed that she was going. Sam waved to her happily. Ellie wasn't sure about the two scantily dressed girls who were draped nearby and gazing at Rick adoringly, but Sam had become much tougher in the last few months, although she too was gazing adoringly at Rick.

Ed the roadie was really nice and they had a couple of coffees each and shared a Mars bar that Ellie found at the bottom of her handbag. She knew that the roadie was off to his new job in the U.S.A. next week ,so it was no use getting too friendly and anyway she decided that she was going to steer clear of men for the time being. Ellie caught a taxi home and Ed pecked her on the cheek and said "bye beautiful girl" This cheered her up no end.

Ellie's mobile woke her with a start. Her mouth was dry and she had a thumping headache.
"Ellie it's me can you pick me up please. " Sam sounded distressed and was crying . Ellie arranged to pick her up outside the hotel and scrambled into some clothes. As Ellie drew up Sam walked quickly out of the hotel, with her hand at the side of her face. Talk about the walk of shame. Her mascara had run down her face, her hair was all over the place and last nights clothes looked distinctively dishevelled.
"Drive off quickly" she muttered "I don't want to be seen."
"are you OK?"
Sam nodded "come on drive quickly. "
Ellie roared off in her mini and then turned to look at Sam who had slithered down in her seat so that no one would see her.
"did you erm with Rick last night?"
Sam nodded again and burst into tears.
"Well fancy not driving you home" said Ellie indignantly.
"he he he would have" sobbed Sam " He was going to send for a car, but he fell asleep and I just wanted to get away. Oh Ellie I'm so ashamed I was like some groupie. I just wanted to feel young and carefree again. It was horrible."
"What did he say?"
"He said 'that was great doll just like the old times. I had a blast" and then he stated screaming down the phone at his agent. When did he start talking like that ? "
"Had a blast !" echoed Ellie and then she started to giggle
"It's not funny" said Sam and then she started to giggle.
"White tulips "gasped Ellie
"When we were in the hotel he demanded a Mexican dish no one had ever heard of " gasped Sam
"and then he said he wanted a new stage backdrop incorporating silver spaceships."

The girls rocked with laughter all the way home.

"I have just realised." said Ellie "We helped with the lyrics for that song. We should probably have a share in the royalties."

" Well I am certainly not going back to ask." squeaked Sam and they laughed again when they imagined Rick's reaction.

"Right that's it I'm finished with men." said Sam as she got out of the car and scurried into the house, hoping none of the neighbours would spot her.

"And me. It's the two musketeers from now on." Ellie shouted as she drove off.

CHAPTER THIRTEEN

The two girls enjoyed themselves over the next few months. On the evenings that Ellie's mum and dad babysat they went to the theatre, cinema and out for meals. Alfie went to bed early and now slept through , so it wasn't a problem for her parents. They also saw quite a lot of live music. They went to a couple of family friendly music festivals and took Alfie. He loved them and would dance around to the music with his mum and aunty Sam, often looking like some kind of animal, as he usually dragged them to the face paint tent. Alfie was a little character. He was full of life and made them laugh . He was quite advanced with his conversation , Ellie thought it was because he was around adults a lot and also Domenica and Stefano. He was a really kind little boy and was always trying to help people.

" Look what I have found mummy. I am going to make him better " was a common cry and he would appear carrying a rescued worm or insect. He loved helping Ellie's mum and dad and on the day that her mum looked after him, she would often find him at the kitchen table, with an apron tied around him while he helped make a cake. It normally involved a large amount of flour judging by the state of the kitchen and of Alfie. He helped her dad in the garden, although she suspected that he was more of a hindrance than help. She saw her dad flinch when Alfie fetched his little wellies to 'help grandad clean out the pond.'

Ellie and Sam borrowed a tent for one festival and camped for two nights. Alfie was in seventh heaven and loved his little sleeping bag . He kept zipping up the bedroom and snuggling inside and then popping out again. Luckily the weather was good.
" Can we live here forever please mummy. " asked Alfie chomping on his cereal as he sat cross legged on a rug outside their tent.
Ellie wiped milk off his chin.
" I don't think you would like it when everyone has gone home and it gets cold in the winter."
"OK" said Alfie after a pause "but this is great. Ooh look mummy there are Pete and Geoff who we were talking to last night."
" Mm yes " replied Ellie trying to hide by the tent and pushing Sam behind her.
Alfie jumped up and ran over to the two men. Pete and Geoff were a couple of older hippy types that they had chatted to briefly the night before. Unfortunately Alfie had taken a shine to them. Alfie led them over

" mummy , aunty Sam, I said that they could share our breakfast as they haven't had any."

Ellie thought that they had probably had breakfast of another sort judging by the smell of weed surrounding them.

" Hey that's really cool of you" beamed Geoff sitting on the grass outside their tent.

Alfie chattered away offering them drinks and cereal and Sam raised her eyebrows at Ellie.

" Have you got husbands or children ?" queried Alfie

" not that we know of " replied Pete.

" Oh good " said Alfie because my mummy hasn't got a husband and Aunty Sam doesn't have her husband any more."

" Careless " smiled Pete

" Mummy had a friend called Xander and I liked him but mummy fell out with him and now I don't have anyone to play football with." He smiled expectantly at Geoff. " mummy can't cook very well, nor can aunty Sam but we can make good cakes."

Ellie looked at Sam in horror, obviously Alfie had taken it upon himself to do a bit of matchmaking. She looked suspiciously at Sam, she was sure she heard a snort and saw her shoulders shaking. They started clearing away as soon as Pete and Geoff had finished and said that they must take Alfie for a shower. Ellie practically pulled Geoff to his feet as it looked as if he was struggling to get up and then her wristband caught in his dreadlocks.

"Oh no I don't want a shower " said Alfie " would you like to come back for some lunch ?"

" he's a trier I will give him that " thought Ellie as she hastily explained that they didn't know where they would be at lunchtime but hoped to see them soon. Pete and Geoff ambled off with a wave and Ellie rounded on Alfie.

" Alfie you can't just ask people to eat with us and try and marry us off " she exclaimed. She could see Sam's shoulders shaking with laughter as she took herself inside the tent and she could hear spluttering noises coming from inside.

Alfie looked up at her and his bottom lip wobbled

" sorry mommy, but I thought you looked a bit sad sometimes now you are not Xander's friend anymore and I thought aunty Sam might want a nice new husband. I didn't really like uncle Ralph" he whispered " you said my daddy works a long way away but he isn't your husband is he ? That's like Mason a big boy who sometimes comes to Valentina's . He has a mummy and a daddy but they live in different houses Mason says and they are not husbands with each other."

Ellie blinked back a tear and pulled him to her and kissed the top of his head.

" well thank you for helping, but aunty Sam and I are quite happy and we don't need husbands. If it's a lady it's called a wife not husband though. We are OK aren't we ? "

Alfie nodded doubtfully. Sam and Ellie spent the rest of the day avoiding Pete and Geoff.

Alfie recovered from his disappointment and enjoyed running around in the dark wearing a glow stick .

"I have stayed up really really late haven't I mummy ? " he whispered when they were all in their sleeping bags " Is it nearly morning ? So is it best not to ask Pete and Geoff to have breakfast with us tomorrow ?"

"NO " yelled two voices

Ellie told them about Alfie when she went back to work

" Honestly his matchmaking is worse than yours" she informed Gemma "and I am not looking on Tinder any more. I have decided that I don't need a man and so has Sam. We have been going to some great places together. "

" After Xander I promised to keep out of your love life " replied Gemma "and as you are not interested you can deal with old Mr Butler who is still looking for a house near his daughter."

" It will be a pleasure." replied Ellie " Hello Mr Butler shall we have a look at what we have available near your Julie's ."

It was a hot day and Ellie decided to go through the drive through at the shopping centre and get one of her favourite frappuccinos. She was chatting to the girl as she handed the drink through the hatch and somehow caught it on the window ledge. A great wave tipped down her shoulder and arm.

" eek not again " she thought as she mopped her blouse. The drink was really cold. She knew there was no one available in the office and so had to meet the next couple with a soggy patch on her front. She used nearly a whole pack of baby wipes and thought it didn't look too bad, it was worse on her shoulder.

"oh well here goes. I wish I could be elegant like the Italian women I see on holiday." she sighed "sorry about my appearance but the last couple had a baby who was a bit sick on me."

The couple smile understandingly , although when they went upstairs at the house they were viewing, Ellie caught the woman sniffing and saying she could smell coffee in a puzzled voice. Ellie dashed home afterwards to change her top. Mark wouldn't have been impressed.

Ellie had managed to save some money which she was hoping to use as a deposit on somewhere of her own. Her parents had told her to stay with them a little longer so that she could buy somewhere rather than rent. It would be easier once Alfie went to the nursery at school as she would be able to increase her hours and hopefully get a mortgage again. Still she mustn't wish his childhood away as he would have to be four to go to nursery and she loved his company. If ever she felt sad he seemed to sense it and would come and sit on her lap with a story book. She always braced herself for a question if there was a child with a daddy but mostly he didn't say anything. One day they were reading about a little girl whose daddy worked far away in India.

" That's like my daddy isn't it " exclaimed Alfie bouncing up and down.

Ellie nodded and smiled.

" and his grandma makes the best tiramisu. I wish I could have some." Alfie sighed wistfully and Ellie felt her eyes fill with tears.

"is she really old mummy ?"

" I don't know Alfie , I never met her. Come on it's nearly bedtime so we need to finish this story." One day she was going to have to give Alfie some sort of explanation about his daddy. Ellie still secretly looked at the photos she had of Dario on her phone, maybe she should show them to Alfie, but not yet.

CHAPTER FOURTEEN

It was Alfies third birthday party and he was beside himself with excitement as three little friends were coming as well as Domenica and Stefano. Valentina had offered to make a cake and Alfie had requested a dinosaur cake. He woke at the crack of dawn and demanded to know if he was three now, like his friend Dylan. Ellie had booked a bouncy castle as a surprise and when the men came and put it up Alfie's face was a picture.

" Can I bounce on it now ? Is it really for me mummy? "

" It is, for you and your friends, but only for today."

Ellie was worried that his little legs would be worn out before the party. She and her parents had had a go and nearly bounced Alfie off into space . Ellie bounced gently after that and held tightly to Alfie's hand. She had been worried that it would be too cold and or wet, that was the trouble having a birthday so late in the year. However it was a cold sunny day and as long as the kids were wrapped up it would be fine. Although she hoped they didn't churn up her dad's lawn.

" Can Dylan bounce on it with me and Stefano and Domenica ? "

" Yes and Darcie and Molly. Now get off it now or you will be too tired to bounce at your party."

" Mummy , mummy can we put some more balloons in the garden. Mummy can I sit next to Stefano please because he is my special friend and Dylan? Mummy will I have some more presents do you think ?"

Ellie sighed as Alfie ran off to supervise his grandad with the balloons, it was going to be a long day, but it was good to see Alfie so excited. He had helped her mum make some colourful cup cakes yesterday, so Ellie took one and sat in the bathroom with it. Bliss five minutes peace.

Sam arrived to help. Alfie ran to her

" Aunty Sam, aunty Sam come and see my balloons and my special digger that mummy bought me."

Sam duly admired the digger and other new toys, any new clothes were of course ignored. Then she sat down and lifted Alfie onto her knee.

"Right before the party starts I have a very special present for you Alfie, but it's for you and mummy , so you need to open it together."

"It's not my birthday for ages" frowned Ellie

"Just shut up and open it. You have been a brilliant friend to me this year and I wanted to treat you out of mum's house sale proceeds, now that it's finally gone through. I am sure I got that extra five thousand pounds due to you insisting on upping Mark's valuation . At the time I wasn't in a mindset to bargain with those buyers, but you were great and I think they really believed that other couple were going to make an offer. Call it an early Christmas present. "

Alfie bounced up and down on Sam's knee with excitement and Ellie helped him open the envelope .

"You can't give us that, it's way too much !" gasped Ellie looking at Sam in shock

"What is it mummy? Mummy what is it ? " Alfie was tugging her sleeve.

"Well Alfie, it says that Aunty Sam is taking us on a skiing holiday after Christmas. It is to a place where they have lots of snow and we will all stay in an hotel together and eat lots of lovely food. "

"Wow thanks Aunty Sam " shouted Alfie jumping up and down and hugging Sam.

"You know I have always wanted to go skiing, well now is my chance." beamed Sam "and I will be going with my two favourite people. You can teach me. Open the other parcel Alfie I have bought you a ski outfit. "

" What's a ski outfit ?"

Alfie wasn't usually interested in clothes, but he took a fancy to the bright red ski suit and insisted on wearing it. He then jumped about pretending to ski.

"I don't think he actually knows what skiing is ! I don't know what to say. Thank you." Ellie felt quite tearful, she hadn't had a holiday since Alfie was born.

" Well Alfie needs to be four to learn, but there is a little creche in the village with a kiddy slope and a little tubing area, so he will have fun there and I can't wait until he is four to do this ! "

" That's brilliant and maybe we can take him on a little slope with us. Alfie I think you need to take that off before your friends come to the party. You are looking a bit red in the face, although it might just be a reflection of your outfit."

Alfie thoroughly enjoyed his party. He told the children all about the skiing holiday and jumped up and down with a bit of sideways wiggle to demonstrate. The children looked confused and ran off to play on the bouncy castle. His face when he blew out the candles on his dinosaur cake was a picture. He couldn't quite manage to blow out the candles in one go and Ellie hated to think what had been sprayed over the cake. They played pass the parcel which was a struggle as only the two older children were willing to actually pass the parcel.

She collapsed exhausted onto the sofa after Alfie had gone to bed and enjoyed a glass or two of wine with Sam and her mum and dad.

"Ooh that's better peace at last."

" I am so glad that you are going on holiday" smiled her mum " It will do you good and it's really kind of you Sam"

" Ellie deserves it and I am relying on her to show me what to do and look after me if I sprain my ankle " she added.

Ellie went shopping with Sam for her outfit.

" It's your turn now. I have tried on my outfit and it's fine, provided I don't have too much hot chocolate and tiramisu when I am there. You will easily be able to spot Alfie and I in our bright red outfits"

" Oh " joked Sam "I heard that calories don't count when you are skiing, because you burn them off."

" Well let's hope it's true." smiled Ellie " now what about this brown jacket, it would really suit you. Get a trolley as you will need quite a few things."

For the first time in ages Ellie had something to look forward to. She had to stop talking about it to Alfie as he had woken her up several times demanding to know if they were going skiing today.

Christmas was lovely as Alfie had now well and truly cottoned on to Santa and presents. They had gone to see Santa in a children's adventure park. The man in queue next to them had chatted and explained that he was divorced and had his two children for the weekend. They saw him again in the playground and Alfie ran around playing with the children. He persuaded Ellie to go to the indoor cafe with the children. He was really pleasant but Ellie's heart wasn't in it. She gave him her mobile number but when he rang the following week she made excuses and put him off.

Alfie was pleased with every present he received and insisted on playing with each present before moving on to the next one. He was especially pleased with his little tractor which was just like Stefano and Domenica's, only smaller. Then he spent many happy hours playing with a large box. He had not been sure about crackers the year before, but now he loved them. Ellie's dad allowed him to pull the rest of the large box of crackers after they had lunch.

" I promised him he could if he ate two sprouts " was the response.

By teatime Alfie was overtired and started crying.

"come on young man. Let's read a few stories and then get you ready for bed . This is what happens when you wake up at four in the morning."

" but I was trying to tell you that Santa had been." exclaimed Alfie crossly and threw the book across the floor

" right bed now !" said Ellie sternly " we don't have that sort of behaviour here , thank you very much."

In the end Alfie was asleep in minutes clutching the rather large spaceman that Uncle Andrew had given him in addition to a spaceship full of little aliens.

It wasn't so bad going back to work after Christmas when there was a holiday to look forward to. Also Ellie was sick of playing spaceships and pulling Alfie along on the tractor. How old were children before they learnt to peddle ?

" You lucky thing going skiing " said Gemma while painting her nails a brilliant red " I wanted to go this year but Mark said we should save for the wedding. I s'pose he's right."

" Are you O.K. ?" queried Ellie " You seem a bit down this week."

" Oh it's just post Christmas blues. I wouldn't mind if we were getting married this year, but we have a whole year and a bit to wait. Also my mum is getting stressed about mother of the bride outfits." She sighed and blew on her fingers.

" Right " said Ellie " you are coming with me at lunchtime. I will treat you to lunch in the pub and you can show me what you have sorted for the wedding so far. Ron will probably give you some tips " she grinned.

"Thanks " said Gemma after lunch , hugging Ellie " That was just what I needed and I am going to leave wedding planning for a while. It's only one day after all."

Ellie had marked the holiday on the calendar in the new year and every morning Alfie would put a squiggle through the day and often a couple more as he wasn't very good at colouring yet.

" Only twenty more days now Alfie. You can count up to twenty can't you ?" Alfie nodded happily and then proceeded to demonstrate, twice, once in English and once in Italian. She was really looking forward to a holiday with her best friend, she probably wouldn't be able to go out in the evenings as she had last time, but it would still be great. Provided she could remember how to ski that is.

"What are you doing mummy? " Alfie's little face peered at her, she was lying on her bedroom floor trying to do some crunches.

" I am just doing some exercises so that I can do the skiing better." She hadn't exercised much since having Alfie. She had even stopped doing the yoga with her mum.

" yay . I will do it too mummy."

Alfie was very enthusiastic but after he nearly gave her a black eye Ellie decided to tickle him instead.

" can I bounce on your bed mummy ? Cos thats sexercise too isn't it mummy?"

The week before they were due to leave Ellie realised she hadn't received any details of the holiday from Sam. She rang her and asked if she could pop over.

" Oh sorry I won't be in " said Sam

"Oh right shall I call in tomorrow after work ? "

"Well it's a bit difficult because I am frantically trying to finish some illustrations before we go. Can we leave it please. I have checked us all in online and have the boarding passes ready to hand you."

" Oh Ok ....well see you on Saturday."

Ellie was a bit disappointed as she was hoping to have a look at the ski brochure to checkout the resort and hotel. It was not like Sam but she must be very busy.

" Only two more sleeps now Alfie."

"yaay" shouted Alfie running around the kitchen like an aeroplane.

CHAPTER FIFTEEN

Ellie's dad was driving them to the airport and Alfie was beside himself with excitement, he had never been on a plane. He had a little pull along suitcase in the shape of a penguin, which his grandparents had bought him for Christmas. He had insisted on packing the penguin that Xander had bought him, although he had finally stopped talking about Xander. Ellie had had to check his case last night as he had taken some things out and added others.

" Alfie you won't need your swimming trunks and armbands. Now don't put anything else in or I will leave it here.".

" Promise mummy .Tell me about the airplane again mummy. You said I could buy a toy one with the pennies I saved from Christmas."

He insisted on Ellie pulling him along through the airport which was a bit of a struggle with all the other luggage. An elegant woman walked past pulling a a small case. Ellie blew the hair off her face and wiped the sweat off her brow. Oh to be glamorous !

Alfie chatted to everyone including security staff, check in ladies , the cabin crew and other passengers and everyone said how cute and well behaved he was. He bought a toy plane and proudly paid with his 'pennies'.

"Mummy , Aunty Sam look out of the window. There are mountains and snow ." He cried excitedly bouncing up and down on his seat. " Look " he unclipped his seatbelt and stood on the seat to shout at the couple behind. "there are mountains, great big mountains with snow and I am going there "
"OK Alfie. sit down now as the people behind might be trying to have a nap."
There was a little girl a few rows in front that Alfie had tried to talk to in the departure lounge. At the time she was too interested in demanding some biscuits from her parents. Ellie had felt quite sorry for her as both parents had been glued to their phones and ignored her until she shouted that she wanted biscuits. Now she had thrown herself in the gangway and was having a full blown tantrum. Alfie looked on in amazement

" what is the matter with that girl mummy, is she hurt ?"

" No Alfie I think she is just being silly because she keeps asking her mummy and daddy to buy her things from the trolley."

" and she is getting them " muttered Sam as the parents thrust toys and crisps at the child

" she is very tired " muttered the father as the child went limp in his arms as he tried to pick her up . She then jerked forward and nutted him in the nose, which elicited more yells from the child and caused a nosebleed for her dad.

"Can't you do anything with her" he said to his wife through gritted teeth. His wife shrugged
" Now you know what I have to put up with every day" and went back to her magazine.
" Hope she is not at our hotel" whispered Sam

Alfie just stared with wide eyes at the girl. Ellie tried to distract him.

When they were waiting for the baggage they saw the father, they knew it was him because of the blood on his shirt, dash forward to stop the little girl climbing on the conveyor belt. His wife was oblivious, she was chatting to another couple. It made Ellie feel less guilty about her single parenthood.

They got on a coach when they landed . Alfie tripped over and bumped his knee on the way to the coach, so Ellie was too busy picking him up and giving him a cuddle to do anything but follow Sam.

"Hold on Alfie I have some wipes in my bag and we will clean you up. Don't touch anything your hands are all muddy."

Sam had taken their hand luggage on board and was waving to them. Alfie was fine after he had been sorted out and chattered all the time and kept looking out of the window for signs of snow. He eventually fell asleep exhausted and Ellie fell asleep too. Sam coughed and it woke Ellie, who looked around and suddenly realised how shifty Sam had been looking. She had not paid much attention to the destinations on the coaches . She wouldn't would she? Ellie glanced at Sam who was now asleep, or at least pretending to be. Snow started to appear at the sides of the road and gradually became thicker as they climbed up the mountain. Ellie gasped as they entered the village, it looked familiar, it was Barganago, Dario's village.

"How could you do this to me? I never dreamt you would choose this place." she turned a shocked white face to Sam.

"I'm sorry I just think you need to sort this out once and for all, for your sake. I don't think you can move on until you do." whispered Sam " Do you hate me?"

"No but I don't like you very much at the moment ."

and Ellie stomped off the coach, holding a sleeping Alfie in her arms. She was absolutely raging mad and couldn't trust herself to speak.

" I will see to the luggage, you go in. " said Sam anxiously.

" Here let me help .",

Sam turned around to see a tall good looking man grinning at her.

" Hi my name is Jack and that's my little sister Sophie. Looks like we are all in the same hotel. " Sam looked at the girl hoisting a case away from the coach. You could tell that they were brother and sister. They were both tall with straight blonde hair. Sophie waved at Sam in a friendly way.

" Thanks " said Sam a little tearfully

' Are you O.K." asked Jack " Only you look a bit upset"

" No I am fine, it's just that I have sprung a surprise on my friend and she's not too happy."

It was even the same hotel and Enzo and Maria greeted Ellie like old friends and carried the bags up to her room whilst she carried a sleeping Alfie , who was wearing a big woolly hat and scarf.

"oh the beautiful bambino" said Maria stroking his cheek. Ellie asked if she could have some food in the room to save disturbing Alfie, as he would sleep until morning after all the excitement. Sam knocked on the door and asked to join her, although Ellie had told her to go to the dining room. There was a stony silence for about half an hour.

"I'm really, really sorry. I was trying to help " blurted Sam " Do you want me to see if we can change to another resort?"

Ellie sighed "No you're right and I'm sorry for being horrible. You did it with my best interests at heart and I think you are right. Dario needs to know he has a son. I think I will try to avoid him and then maybe speak to him or leave him a note or something towards the end of the holiday. It's not as if I want any maintenance or anything from him, but maybe he should know about Alfie. You go down to the bar "

" No it's all right I need an early night. Besides I don't know anyone."

" Didn't I see a handsome young man helping with our bags? "

Sam blushed " He was rather nice wasn't he. He said he is here with his sister. I will go down and get us a glass of wine. is that O.K. ?" she asked anxiously

Ellie nodded and then went into the bathroom for a little cry. It looked like their lovely holiday was ruined, she would need to spend all her time avoiding Dario.

Alfie was still fast asleep but Ellie hardly slept that night , she kept tossing and turning. When dawn broke she crept out of bed to gaze at Alfie. He was so gorgeous with his long dark lashes sweeping his chubby cheeks. His hair grew upwards from the corner of his forehead, just like Dario's.
"Well little man your daddy will soon find out about you. Will he want to meet you or have nothing to do with you ? He might be married with children by now. Never mind if he doesn't want us we will manage. We have for three years haven't we ? "
A tear trickled down her cheek and Ellie swiped it away angrily. She had avoided this for so long. She had had a horrible feeling in the pit of her stomach since they drove into the village. Ellie didn't think she would be able to enjoy the holiday, but she would put on a brave face for Alfie and Sam. Eventually she got up and had a shower and carefully put away their clothes.

Alfie woke up full of beans and had to look in all the cupboards and little bathroom.
" we are sharing aren't we mummy, like a sleepover. Ooh mummy there is snow outside and big big mountains."
Ellie had forgotten that he had fallen asleep before they reached the village. She wrapped her arms around him and they gazed out of the window.
"There is snow on everythink " breathed Alfie "even on that car an' the mountain , everywhere." he threw his arms out wide and clunked Ellie on the head " Come on let's go and tell aunty Sam about the snow." They knocked on Sam's door and went down to breakfast together, Alfie holding Sam's hand and chattering. Sam was relieved that Ellie had accepted that she needed to see Dario. Sam loved Alfie so much and just knew that Dario couldn't fail to love him once he met him.

When Maria saw Alfie without his hat, she dropped the basket of bread she was holding and got very flustered. The other members of the party were lovely and made a fuss of Alfie. There were two glamorous girls called Chloe and Poppy and a couple Sean and Phil , who were all good skiers. The brother and sister Jack and Sophie would be joining the beginners group with Sam. They were all really friendly and made Alfie laugh.
" Don't I have to have porridge or weetabix here mummy. Can I really have cake?"
Alfie's bright blue eyes were wide with wonder.
"As long as you have a yoghurt and a banana."
" cool this is great isn't it mummy ?"

" Oh he is so cute " said Poppy pinching his cheek and then quickly wiping her hand on a tissue. Alfie did have yoghurt all over his face.

" Honestly " said Sam when they went up to their rooms " Chloe and Poppy are so glamorous. They are both wearing full make up and false eyelashes "

" and did you see their nails ?" squeaked Ellie " there were even fake diamonds on the ends ! We are going to look so scruffy next to them."

" They seem lovely though and at least we are natural. Now tell me what I have to take to ski school. I feel really nervous."

" Just your boots, skis, helmet and lift pass. I would come with you but I don't know which instructor you will have. I can't face Dario today. Don't worry you will have the lovely Jack to help you." Sam thwacked her with her gloves.

" Come ON ! " said a little voice " I want to see the snow an' I have waited ages "

While the beginners went off together Ellie took Alfie to the creche. When she walked out of the door Enzo looked at Maria and said "Dario" she nodded and said "Alfreddo" and went into the back to make a phone call. Alfie ran ahead and shouted

" Look mummy , look at the snow, there's lots and lots and lots of it." and he scooped some up and threw it at Ellie.

" Don't pick up the snow now or your hands will get really cold, even with your gloves on.. Wait until later when we get back by the hotel and we will have a snowball fight."

" Promise ?"

" Promise"

" I can kick it though can't I ? " He happily kicked piles of snow all the way to the centre of the village. He fell into the snow a couple of times and thought it was hilarious.

Ellie was nervous about leaving him at the creche, but after watching him for ten minutes she could see he was really enjoying himself. There were loads of toys inside and out. There was a little tubing and sledging slope and playground. There was also a little kitchen and they provided the children with drinks and snacks.

" Wow" Alfie's eyes were as round as saucers. He went and joined some children, who were all wearing brightly coloured snow clothes.

" we have a room where they can rest and have a little sleep." said the nursery lady " but usually they too busy."

"I will collect you for lunch and we will meet aunty Sam." she shouted but Alfie just waved and carried on chattering in Italian to his new little friends. Thank goodness there was no language barrier as most of the children were Italian.

Ellie fastened her boots and clicked on her skis.
" Here goes let's hope I remember what to do." Amazingly she did and had a quiet morning on the easy slopes, getting her ski legs and looking out for Dario so that she could avoid him. She thought she saw him once and ducked behind a group having a lesson. She was a nervous wreck by the time she finished for lunch. She had enjoyed skiing at her own pace instead of following a line of others in a group.

Ellie picked up Alfie and he demanded that she watch him go down the small slope on a sledge.
"Can I come back tomorrow" he pleaded " I love it here."
"Yes " she laughed. The staff were impressed by his Italian
"Is better than my English" one remarked.

They met Sam for lunch and Jack and Sophie asked if they could join them. They had enjoyed their lesson which had been taken by a charming instructor called Giovanni.
"He told us to call him Gio." said Sam beaming happily. "We all had to step up the slope sideways at first but then he took us on the travelator."
" Yes and we all fell over lots of times " added Jack, he seemed to like Sam and it looked as though the feeling was mutual, although in a lovely easy going way, not the way it had been with Ralph. Jack and his sister were both blonde . Jack's hair stood up in tufts when he removed his ski helmet. Sophie teased him and ruffled his hair.
" Just look at the state of your hair ! Ellie what are you doing under the table ?"
Ellie was sure she had seen Dario walk into the restaurant with some other ski instructors .
" Nothing " came a muffled voice from under the table " I think something fell out of my pocket." she scrambled back onto the chair and kept her head bent. The others looked at her a bit strangely. They all insisted on looking after Alfie while she had a quick ski on the longer run . Ellie left as quickly as she could, putting her helmet on first and keeping her head down. She felt hot all over

and was trembling. If she did bump into him, she didn't want to see him looking like this. After a while she skied back to the restaurant and peered inside. It had emptied out a lot and she could see Alfie and the others.

" Thank you so much I really enjoyed that ."

Alfie had chocolate all around his face.

"What have you been eating guzzle guts " demanded Ellie poking him the ribs.

"Hot choclit " replied Alfie giggling "with a snowy mountain on top. It was deeelicious."

"Well done " Ellie muttered " you haven't done badly for someone who always says he hates cream." She left them to have a little practice while she took Alfie back to the hotel.

They walked back down the hill, Alfie chattering happily and Ellie glancing around to make sure Dario was nowhere in sight. She heard a voice behind her and jumped and turned around quickly and promptly fell over. The man and Alfie had to help her up. Alfie thought it was funny.

" Typical" thought Ellie " I never fell over once skiing." What with that and the snowball fight on the way back, she didn't look very elegant by the time they got back to the hotel. Alfie had to be bribed to go back inside, he was having so much fun.

"But I don't want a nap" Alfie shouted and thrust out his bottom lip and stamped his foot." I am NOT tired" Ellie raised her eyebrows.

" You sound like that little girl on the plane, so you can cut that out right now. If you have a nap you can stay up late and have dinner with mummy and Aunty Sam."

"and Jack and Sophie and Sean and Phil?"

"yes "

Alfie thought that was a good idea, as he wanted to eat his dinner in the dark with his new friends like a grown up. After two Peppa Pig stories he was soon fast asleep. Ellie had a nap too as she hadn't slept well the night before. Sam came back and tapped on the door and woke Ellie.

" What do you think of Jack?" she whispered

"he is really nice, but I thought you were off men!"

Sam shrugged "I really enjoyed the lesson and can't wait until tomorrow when we go on a proper lift with our skis. I fell over a few times and he rushed to help me up. He doesn't live far away and his sister is lovely. I know, I know I have only just met him, but it feels different this time. I just wish you were happier."

"I am fine and I am quite happy to eat Maria's gorgeous food and sit in front of the fire. It's such a treat."

Sam went back to her room to try on her outfits for dinner.

"jeans, jeans or jeans really " she smiled.

Ellie had a shower and washed her hair, removing bits of twigs which seemed to have found their way into Alfie's snowballs. What should she wear ? She wasn't going out but that didn't mean she couldn't look nice for their evening meal. She chose a new blue sweater that she had bought. Alfie was in a much better mood after a long nap and they sat in the bedroom and played a game they had brought with them. He was wearing a new pair of jeans and a red sweatshirt with snowflakes on which he had insisted on bringing, with Christmas socks.

" I really really like it here mummy."

" Good " smiled Ellie " remember to tell Aunty Sam because she bought us this holiday." Alfie nodded " I love Aunty Sam best in the world after you and gran and grandad." he wriggled his toes

" Is it nearly time for dinner 'cos I'm really hungry ?"

" Not just yet, but lets go down to the bar because I think Maria will have made some snacks for us. Pick up the game, we can play it by the fire. Now go and tap on Aunty Sam's door." The rooms all had lovely old wooden doors and there were lots of paintings of the mountains lining the corridor. The light switches had to be pressed and the lights would go on for a short time. Alfie thought this great fun and made them wait a while so that the lights went off when they were part way down the stairs.

"We are all going to fall, put the light back on Alfie! "

Alfie was really well behaved at dinner. He had taken a shine to Sean and Phil and asked if he could sit by them. They were delighted and kept Alfie entertained and showed him a magic trick. After dinner he followed Maria and Enzo around chattering in English. Ellie realised that he only spoke in Italian, if someone spoke to him in Italian, that made sense. They all sat around the log fire and had a drink. Chloe and Poppy had obviously spent ages on their hair. They both had streaked blond hair, with extensions that fell in artful waves down their back. Their nails were works of art. Sometimes Ellie thought that she must be the only person who had never had a manicure. It sounded as if they were quite well off and kept referring to other ski holidays they had been on around the world.

" I was only four when I learned to ski." Poppy informed Alfie " so you will be able to learn next year." Alfie nodded excitedly.

" Not much chance of that " thought Ellie and smiled politely

" honestly he is soo gorgeous " said Poppy patting him on the head. She and Chloe were off in search of male company. Sean kindly read one of Alfie's stories to him, with sound effects made by Phil. Alfie loved it. They then went to explore the village and asked the others to join them.

"You go" Ellie said to Sam "I am quite happy here reading my book. In fact I might go to bed when Alfie does. I didn't sleep too well last night."

"It's my fault, isn't it ?" demanded Sam.

"No it isn't . You are right , I need to sort this out for Alfie's sake. You go with them. You might slip on the ice and need Jack to pick you up again."

"sshh" replied Sam blushing "he might hear you are you sure ? I don't like to leave you."

"Sure, now go on"

Ellie saw Sophie link arms with Sam and Jack and was relieved that Sam was getting a chance to socialise again.

It was lovely and cosy by the fire and Alfie kept running up to show them the toy cars that Enzo had found for him to play with. He hadn't bothered with the game.

"There is a great big box mummy" said Alfie with eyes as big as saucers and Enzo said I can play with them while I am staying here. When we go home I can pick one to keep forever. I fink it might be this one, or this one . " and off he dashed to have another look.

" Grazie " mouthed Ellie to Enzo , who smiled

"eez no problem . They belong to my son Patrizio who is now ski instructor."

Ellie sat sipping her wine and leafing through a magazine. Enzo had taken Alfie out the back to show him a special digger he had found, bliss. She felt her eyes drooping…

" Maria you left message for me to come. Maria .." someone shouted

Ellie froze, she would recognise that voice anywhere. She slowly turned around.

"Ellee" Dario looked shocked . He walked over to her

" I did not know you were here. Maria she left a message for me to come." then he recovered himself

" um hello are you here for skiing ?" he said frostily. His eyes were cold and angry and not like the old Dario, although he looked as handsome as ever . He turned to walk away. Ellie felt her heart turn over, but she suddenly felt all the anger and hurt return.

"Why do you want to say hello now ? You couldn't be bothered saying goodbye last time. Are they short of women at ski school this week ? "

Dario looked puzzled .

"What you mean?"

Ellie jumped up , her cheeks were flaming and she had tears of anger in her eyes.

"I mean that after you had your wicked way with me, several times, " she added huffily " you left while I was asleep and I never heard from you again. I suppose you moved on to the next girl as I was leaving the next day ! "

She had to get away from him, where was Alfie.

"Wait" Dario grabbed her arm and turned her around to face him "You mean when I left. I sent you note and then I tried to ring you and I texted many many times , but you no reply."

"What note?"

"I gave that girl .. er Gabriella a note. My grandfather he was very ill and I was called to the hospital, he died that night."

Ellie looked at him in horror, shocked as she realised what had happened to Dario that morning.

" I , I didn't get a note. I thought you didn't care, after what Gabriella said to me, that I was just another....oh I lost my phone in the airport. I am so sorry about your grandfather, if I had known I would..."

"You would ..what?"

"I would have tried to contact you."

He shrugged "It is long time ago, I gave it to Gabriella I expect you have forgotten me . What did she say to you ? I meant what I said then. I do not how you say "move on" to different girl each week. I told you that " He looked angry now, waved his hands in the air and started to leave again.

" Wait ! I have never forgotten you Dario. I asked Gabriella where you were and she said you were giving a private lesson to some blond girl and said ' you know what he is like .' The bitch ! "

Dario stood still for a moment and then shook his head in anger. "

"Why ? why she do that to us ?"

" Because she was jealous and wanted you for herself I expect. " said Ellie in small voice. She had been so wrong. He would hate her now. She looked up and they gazed into each others eyes and Dario said

" so maybe we can see each other now . Yes ?" and he smiled his wonderful Dario smile and Ellie promptly melted. She nodded as she couldn't speak, just as a small volcano erupted into the room in the form of Alfie.

"Look mummy, see what Enzo has made me." and he flashed a tiny sword made of cardboard.

Dario glanced at Alfie in surprise and backed away

"I am sorry I will go . I did not think , I expect you are married, sorry."

He knocked over the chair as he turned to leave and Ellie grabbed his jacket, she could see tears in his eyes as he turned around.

"no wait, please. I'm not married, never have been. Sit down I would like to introduce you to someone. This is Alfie. "

"Alfie? " Dario looked at Alfie properly.

" Hi " Alfie wriggled off her knee and ran back to Enzo, giving Dario a cheeky wave.

Dario looked after Alfie and then back at Ellie.

"Is, is he mine?" he whispered.

Ellie nodded the tears running down her face

"Well he is your double. I'm sorry I didn't think you cared ." she sobbed

Dario couldn't speak tears were dripping off his face

"A son, my son, you have had my son ! I am so sorry I should have tried to find you. I thought you only wanted a holiday romance when you not answer my texts. There has never been anyone that mattered since you. I couldn't stop thinking about my lovely English Girl."

"me neither" sobbed Ellie " I tried not to but I kept thinking about you."

and then they were hugging and kissing each other. After about ten minutes Alfie wandered into the room looking really tired. Ellie realised that Enzo and Maria had been keeping him out of the way whilst the drama unfolded.

Ellie sat him on her lap. He looked at her

"mummy have you been crying?" he asked sternly.

"just a little bit because I am so happy. Remember mummy told you that you did have a daddy but he lived a long way away? "

Alfie nodded solemnly "In Italy because he has to work"

"Well your daddy lives here and this is your daddy. Would you you like to give him a hug?"

Alfie stared at Dario in wonder for a while and then jumped down and gave him a hug, more tears slid down Dario's face.

"Hello daddy are you crying cus you are happy too?"

Dario smiled and nodded unable to speak.

"OK will you come up with mummy and read me a bedtime story?"

Dario nodded and found his voice

"I would love to read a story to my little boy."

Just then Maria appeared and said

"two peas in a pod and just like Alfreddo" and started to cry. Enzo came to join her and also shed a tear

"mummy people in Italy cry a lot don't they."

Alfie was tucked up in bed fast asleep and Ellie and Dario sat side by side watching him and holding hands.

"Did you name him for my grandfather?" Dario whispered. Ellie nodded

"Although I called him Alfie not Alfreddo on the birth certificate. I did name you on the birth certificate." she said anxiously "Is that OK?"

"More than OK. I am the luckiest man. I have found you again and I have a son. I am not letting you go this time." He leant over and kissed her gently on the lips. Ellie felt the familiar swirling sensation. Yes Dario was definitely 'the one ' and she was happy that she hadn't accepted a substitute. The thought that she might have settled down with Xander and never seen Dario again and Dario might never have met Alfie filled her with horror. She burst into tears

" sshh you will wake Alfie. What is it? " Dario cradled her gently and she told him everything that had happened since she had last seen him.

"I am so sorry " she hiccuped.

" Is no matter , we are together now. I also went out with other girls, but none of them were my Ellie." He wiped her tears away gently and kissed her again and again.

They slept in each others arms and Dario woke her to say he was going to ski school and could he meet them at lunchtime. Alfie woke not long after Dario had left.

" Where is my daddy ? Has he gone away again." his little voice wavered.

" No, no your daddy stayed with you all night and we are going to meet him at lunchtime . He had to go to work as he is a ski instructor."

" Is that why he could't come and see me then."

Ellie hugged Alfie fiercely.

" yes but also because he didn't know he was your daddy. So it's not his fault is it ? Now he knows he will see you lots and lots."

Alfie beamed and clapped his hands.

" I've got a daddy now, I've got a daddy. I'm going to tell Aunty Sam. Come on I'm hungry."

Ellie went down to breakfast with a beaming smile and Alfie ran up to Sam

" Aunty Sam, aunty Sam I saw my daddy last night and guess what he does .. he is a ski instructa and has to work very hard." and he skipped off to the buffet

Sam looked at Ellie in horror but Ellie just grinned back at her.

" It's fine it was just a big misunderstanding " and she explained it all to Sam and then hugged her

" Thank you for making me come " and she shed another tear

Sam clapped her hands in delight and shared the story with the rest of the dining room.

"That is so romantic" sighed Sean

"and he is fab" said Chloe, "I saw him at ski school yesterday, although we have found a gorgeous instructor called Antonio who is taking Poppy and I out today. We want to explore further afield. Poppy and I might have to fight over him. " Poppy smiled

"I think he is definitely a ' love 'em and leave them ' type, but that suits me. I need a holiday romance."

"Well you never know what it might lead too" teased Sam and Ellie noticed Jack smiling at Sam with a besotted look on his face,"

" Come on sleepyhead time for our lesson. " said Sophie , digging her brother in the ribs

"Shall we meet you in the ski room in ten minutes Sam ?" Sam nodded and they all started making a move.

Sam gave Maria a hug

"Thank you for looking after Alfie last night."

Maria returned the hug " I am so 'appy you and Dario are together. He been very sad after you left. He tell me what happened when I see him this morning. That Gabriella she no good. When I saw

Alfie at breakfast yesterday I realise who 'is daddy is and I telephone Dario and say I need to see him in bar, but I no tell 'im about you and little Alfie. "

" Thank you. I was not brave enough to tell him myself in case he didn't want Alfie."

" course he want the beautiful bambino." said Maria looking sternly at Ellie " he look like 'is papa but 'e also look like Alfreddo. His nonna will be so 'appy."

Alfie asked when he would be seeing his daddy again and wanted to know if his daddy was coming home with them. Ellie didn't have an answer to that. He skipped into the creche and told the ladies that he was meeting his daddy for lunch ,who was a 'ski instucta' Ellie didn't think they believed him and she wasn't up to explaining. Ellie had a lovely long ski, the snow was perfect and she found that skiing on her own she could relax into her own rhythm and not keep stopping. She admired the view and stopped at a mountain restaurant for a hot chocolate. she sat in the sun sipping her drink with a smile on her face. The sun was quite warm, she was glad that she had smothered herself and Alfie with suncream. She went down one slope that had big chunks of snow at the side, hit one, wobbled and fell over. It took a while for her to put on the ski that a passing skier had kindly retrieved for her and the decided to finish for lunch and go and collect Alfie. He wanted her to watch him and his new friend Marco on the tubes. Ellie clapped them twice and then took him to the ski school. She had dreaded meeting Gabriella as she thought she might slap her, but Dario said she had left after one year, which was just as well as he also felt the same way. He also said that nobody had liked her much and there had been complaints from the customers.

"That woman she kept you and Alfie from me all this time. I so angry !"

"Come on Alfie we are going to meet daddy at ski school." She then had to explain to Alfie what ski school was. He had been to school to collect the children with Valentina and had thought it was like that.

Ellie felt nervous walking into the ski school. What would they think of her ? Alfie ran ahead and Dario welcomed them both with a beaming smile and proudly showed off his son. The instructors lifted Alfie onto the counter and made a fuss of him while they chatted.

"I rang my mamma and told her everything," he said "she cried and she and my father and grandmother want to meet both of you . My mama she say….."

Suddenly he stopped talking and listened to Alfie talking.

" 'e is speaking Italian." he said in wonder. Ellie nodded

"well his daddy is Italian!"

Dario got choked up again and hugged her and hugged Alfie.

"Thank you. He can speak to my nonna now."

"Are you crying again daddy?"

They all laughed.

" you speak Italian like me which is very good. We have to do something about that terrible Roman accent though." and he tickled Alfie

" I have learnt more Italian too " smiled Ellie

Dario raised his eyebrows

" good you will be able to speak to my nonna too."

" What is the matter ? " he frowned

" Nothing. I am just a bit scared of meeting your family."

" No they will love you, like me." and he kissed her

" Ugh soppy " said a little voice

Dario grinned and produced a little pair of skis.

" we have lunch and then I teach you to ski, before my next lesson."

" Yay really daddy I thought I had to be four."

" Not when your daddy knows all right people. "

" come on mummy finish your lunch. Me and daddy want to go skiing."

Alfie was shoving pasta into his mouth at a rate of knots

" slow down Alfie you will be sick, you are 'alf Italian now and we do not eat quickly."

Alfie immediately slowed down and nodded his head.

" I am a bit Italian aren't I ? I am going to tell Stefano and Domenica that I am like them now." he smiled at a passing man and said ' ciao '

Alfie walked proudly by Dario who was carrying Alfie's little skis over his shoulder with his own. Dario took him to the nursery slope , which had a little travelator so that beginners didn't have to keep walking up and down the slope. Ellie watched and thought her heart would burst with joy. She took loads of videos and sent them to her mum and dad. At the end of the lesson Alfie was beside himself.

" I can ski now mummy like you and daddy . We can all ski together when I am a bit bigger."

" He is really good " grinned Dario " he follow his papa "

" cheeky, how do you know it's not me " smiled Ellie poking him with a ski pole.

They waved to Dario and went back to the hotel.

" I think you need a nap after all this excitement young man"

Alfie nodded happily

" I love skiing mummy . I want to stay here forever with you and daddy ."

That's going to be one big problem thought Ellie.

" come on we are going to meet Aunty Sam for a hot chocolate and maybe some cake before your nap . Aunty Sam has been learning to ski too. Do you think she is as good as you ?"

Alfie shook his head

" No I think I am the bestest because my daddy teached me. Can I have a hot chocolate with a mountain on like before?"

"I expect so if Aunty Sam hasn't gobbled up all the chocolate cake, like mountains now do you ? Come on I'll race you."

They arrived at the little cafe laughing and sweaty.

"Just look at all these delicious cakes" groaned Sam " how can we resist."

"We don't " replied Ellie "remember all the calories we have been burning off."

"ooh can I have this one ?" shouted Alfie " No I think this one's better, or maybe this one."

The man behind the counter was laughing at Alfie and gave him a lollypop when he left.Alfie quickly went to sleep, Ellie thought he was probably in some sort of chocolate coma. While he was asleep she had a nap as it had been an eventful few days, with a lifetime of adventure ahead she thought smiling.

She was woken by Sam tapping the door.

"It's a good thing you woke us as I think we might have slept through."

"Just look at you"Sam exclaimed " I haven't seen you this happy for ages."

" and its all thanks to you ' said Ellie hugging her tearfully.

CHAPTER SIXTEEN

In the meantime Sam was having a wonderful holiday. She, Jack and Sophie were getting on like a house on fire and enjoying their lessons. Ellie didn't have to worry about Sam in the evenings as she was going out with the rest of the crowd from the hotel. They were all great company. Ellie would meet Sam in the afternoon before they went back to the hotel and they would have a hot chocolate or vin brûlée and cake at their coffee shop in the village. Alfie was a favourite, due to his cheeky smile and Italian chatter. The staff would come around the counter to pick him up and give him a hug and a kiss and he would leave with a pocket stuffed full of sweets. One afternoon they took him around the counter and let him squirt cream on their hot chocolates. He was a bit enthusiastic and squirted cream on the man's arm.

" Hey look what you done to me" and he placed a dollop on Alfie's nose. Alfie started laughing and laughed so much he got hiccups.

"you are going to have trouble with him when he is older " remarked Sam, watching one of the customers pressing some euros into his hot little hand.

"I know but he is having the time of his life. Thank you. Oh look there's Poppy and Chloe."

The two girls were walking each side of their very handsome instructor. He flashed his dazzling white teeth, when they waved to the girls.

" Quick put your sunglasses on so we look more glamorous " said Sam " phew he looks a handful."
" I think our ladies are quite capable of looking after themselves."

The two girls Chloe and Poppy were man mad and flirted with any available man. They were always heavily made up but were sweet and very kind to Alfie. Chloe was a bit dippy and sometimes came out with some howlers. On the first evening she was asked if she wanted a digestif after her meal, which was a liqueur to help with digestion. This had been explained to them by the rep. Chloe had recoiled in horror and she said that she never ever ate biscuits and didn't the waiter think they had eaten enough. In fact neither of them ate very much and Maria was always trying to get them to eat more. On the other hand they drank an awful lot of prosecco.

Ellie had introduced Sam to Dario when he came to the hotel after dinner. He had hugged Sam
" Thank you for bringing Ellie and Alfie 'ere. I can never thank you enough." He pulled away from her with tears in his eyes. "So are you here with your 'usband ?"
Ellie was madly shaking her head at him, but he didn't see.

" No Ralph and I are divorced. Thank goodness " she added.

Dario beamed " aah good "e no good for you. I remember Ellie tell me about 'im. I find you a good Italian man. Yes ? "

Ellie laughed "I think you are too late Dario " and she smiled at Sam, who blushed.

" I really like him " whispered Sam when Alfie had dragged him off to look at something. " you can tell he is madly in love with you . He is perfect for you and Alfie. You were right to wait . I have been talking to Sam and telling him about some of the things Ralph used to say. He was horrified. I can't believe that I put up with it for so long. I can tell that Sam is totally different, I bet his mum and dad are lovely too. I bet you can't wait to meet Dario's parents."

Ellie smiled tightly, it was not something she was looking forward too,

Alfie was always getting someone to read him a story. Ellie told them that they didn't have to but they insisted that they enjoyed it, sometimes there was a little tussle as to who would do it. In fact he was getting spoiled by the whole hotel. There was a little shop nearby which had a selection of toy cars and every so often someone would say

" come on Alfie, come with me to the shop and choose a car " They were not going to have any room in their cases at this rate. Sean and Phil were particular favourites as they had an extensive knowledge of vehicles. Alfie was impressed by their knowledge of diggers in particular.

" you do much better voices than me when you read to him " smiled Ellie.

" well he has helped us make our mind up " said Phil beaming " when we get home we are going to put in an application to adopt. We have been thinking about it for a while, but this time with Alfie has made us realise that it is what we want. We just hope we get a child as wonderful as Alfie. He is a credit to you."

Ellie felt quite tearful. Alfie merely rolled his eyes at her and requested another story from Sean.

Both girls were still chasing their ski instructor Antonio who was Swiss. He was even better looking close up, in fact too good looking with streaked blond hair and whiter than white teeth which didn't look real and manicured eyebrows. He looked as if he could be wearing some man make up.

"Too good looking for his own good " muttered Sam

"Oh Antonio is so sweet" breathed Chloe tossing back her hair. " Poppy and I booked him for private lessons every afternoon and he is marvellous. He leaves us at the bar at the top of the mountain. You know the one near the border with Switzerland with the fabulous cocktails. He says we should have a rest so that we are not too tired to party with him." she giggled "and then he goes up to the shrine to meet Jesus, bless, he seems very religious. We are going again tomorrow. It's a brilliant run back to the village. He knows all the best bars and clubs too."

Ellie asked Dario about Antonio. He said he didn't really know Antonio, as he had only come to the village this season.
" He is very friendly but I think he is, how you say Lazy ? He doesn't come to the bar with the rest of us, he always with the pretty girls. He always seem to have plenty of money . Maybe his family in Switzerland they rich " and he shrugged

Sam went to a bar with live music with the others and Dario and Ellie decided to sit round the fire with Alfie and then put him to bed together. Alfie loves Dario and follows him everywhere. Ellie kept hearing "daddy come here, daddy watch me do this, daddy carry me on your shoulders" and Dario would do whatever he asked.
" I am going to go home with one spoiled brat " sighed Ellie.
He had taken Alfie to nonno Alfreddo's house. Alfie was entranced and inspected all the photos. Dario patiently explained who everyone was and said " Alfie do you know you are named after my nonno Alfreddo ? He was a very good skier and a ski instructor like me."
" I am going to be a good skier like you and nonno daddy an' I'm going to be a ski instructa too. " he frowned "what will I do in the summer daddy? I know I will be a builder with diggers." and he ran off to inspect 'his bedroom' at daddy's house. He had made himself at home and decided where he would stay next time they visited. Dario laughed and asked him what colour he would like it painted.
They would talk and make love all evening whilst Alfie slept . Ellie had never felt so at peace. She would wake up in the night and gaze at Dario and Alfie.
"stop it Ellie "
"What ?"
" You are doing that thing again, Looking at me when I asleep."
"That's because I can't believe that I have found you again. I need to pinch myself, or maybe I should pinch you." she pinched Dario and shrieked when he chased her into the bathroom, where they made passionate love in the shower.
"Why you keep covering your stomach with towel ?" enquired Dario

"because I still have some wobbly bits "
"wobbly bits, wobbly bits, what is this wobbly bits? This is what made our beautiful son ," and he whipped the towel off Ellie and started kissing her wobbly bits.

Maria spoke to Ellie the next morning
"I have never seen Dario so 'appy and wait 'til his parents and nonna see him. " and she wiped a tear from her eye.
Sam came down to breakfast holding Jack's hand. Ellie raised her eyebrows and Sam blushed.
"I know I said I was off men " she whispered "but he is fantastic and I have fallen madly in love with him. I was a fool to ever think I loved Ralph or Rick. He makes me laugh and he is so kind, he never puts me down. Sophie is brilliant too. Sometimes you know Sophie reminds me of someone but I can't think who."
"good you deserve some happiness" Ellie said giving her a big hug. "Now can you spare time to meet me for a coffee and tiramisu later. I want to talk to you about what I should do next."
Sam nodded happily and proceeded to pile her plate high with jam, bread, croissants and several yoghurts. She caught Ellie raising her eyebrow and grinned.
"I don't know why but I am really hungry today."

Ellie and Dario had several conversations about their future. Dario wanted her to move to Italy.
"Lets just see how things go" Ellie explained that they hadn't known each other long and he might find that he didn't like her. Dario looked deeply into her eyes and said
"my heart know you and I know you. I have waited long time for you and I am not letting you go again."
Ellie had never felt so happy, she felt that they were a complete little family now. She was a bit worried about what his family would say and whether they would be angry with her for keeping Alfie away from them for three years. She felt angry that Dario had been deprived of seeing Alfie as a baby. Every day Dario squeezed in a short lesson with Alfie and Ellie could see that he was a natural. One evening he said that he would cook for them at his house .
" but I not have tiramisu this time " he said with a twinkle
" never mind daddy. Do you have any gelato ? "
Alfie loved exploring his great grandfather's house and begged to stay the night. In the end Ellie texted Sam to let her know and they all slept in Alfreddo's house. Dario's bed was the comfiest bed

she had ever slept in. Although the front of the house looked over the village street the back had a wonderful view of the mountains. The next morning she opened the window and sat gazing at the view. This could be her view every day. Alfie woke up and joined her, Dario was already in the kitchen making coffee. He had to be at ski school for an early lesson. Ellie and Alfie walked back to the hotel for breakfast as Alfie was concerned that Dario had no cake.

Sam had confided in Ellie that things with her and Jack had become serious and she thought that she would ask Jack to move in with her when they returned.
" I will wait for a little while first " she added when Ellie looked concerned " but I am really, really sure this time."
Ellie hoped so, especially if she would be seeing less of her best friend. Sam was enjoying the skiing and she, Jack and Sophie would go for a practice ski after lunch.
" I think we are getting better because it used to take over an hour to get down the slope back to the village and we managed it in twenty minutes today and that's with Sophie getting tangled up in the netting at the side of the slope. You should have seen us, I went to help Sophie and fell over, Jack turned around to see where we were and he fell over. There were three of us scattered over the slope. I nearly wet myself laughing." Sam's eyes sparkled and she looked so different to the way she looked when she was with Ralph.

Sophie had gone to another bar with the others and Sam and Jack were sitting by the fire chatting to Ellie and Dario. Jack and Dario got on well together and had a shared love of old cars. Sam looked so happy, Ellie hoped that their relationship would continue when they returned home. Jack did not live far away.
"Let me show you my pride and joy " he beamed scrolling through his phone. "There she is Mildred" and he showed Dario who was duly impressed and then passed the phone to Sam.
Sam saw a photo of an old red mg sports car. "Great I can see I'm going to have to buy a headscarf." she grinned
"and this is the family" said Jack. Sam looked at the photo, gave a strangled cry and ran out of the room.
"What's the matter with Sam?" asked Ellie rushing over to Jack. He shrugged looking worried
"I really don't know. I hope I didn't upset her by reminding her of her mum."

" I shouldn't think so" frowned Ellie "Here let me see"

Ellie looked at the photo smiled and then she rushed out of the room.

"Don't worry. we'll be back soon."

Ellie rushed up to Sam's room and opened the door. Sam was face down on the bed sobbing.

"Hey, hey it's O.K." said Ellie rubbing her back.

Sam sat up " No, no it's not. I, I ,really liked Jack. I know we haven't known each other very long, but I've never felt this way about anyone. I really love him and thought we had a future together and now I've shagged my brother."

" No you haven't you chump. He's not your brother or any other relation, other than your Dad's stepson and your half sister's half brother."

"Oh yes" gulped Sam as her sobs subsided " I panicked when I saw my dad on the photo. I hadn't any idea his name was Jack as dad calls him J "

"Yes I think I heard Sophie calling him J the other day."

Sam brightened "so that means Sophie is my half sister and I can still go out with Jack. I must have met them both when I was younger, before mum found out. I have visited dad and his wife a few times since mum died , but Jack and Sophie were never there. I was supposed to meet ' J ' and Sophie when I go back."

" Well you have beaten them to it and you will have lovely in laws. Come on let's go back down, Jack is panicking and I hate to think what Alfie is doing."

" No wonder Sophie looks familiar, she is a bit like Dad isn't she ? "

" Now you come to mention it I can see the likeness and she is a bit like you, with a lot of Jack thrown in. "

" Do you think so. Oh I do wish we could have grown up together. Maybe not because then Jack would be like a real brother."

Jack looked up in concern "Are you O.K.? I didn't mean to upset you."

Sam nodded, sat on his lap and kissed his cheek.

" Sorry to be so dramatic, it was just a shock. I've got my phone would you like to see my dad?"

Jack nodded and looked confused taking the phone she proffered

"But that's my stepdad" then his face cleared "Sam, of course! What are the chances? I can see why you were shocked. This won't spoil anything will it?"

Sam shook her head " It freaked me out for a while. I thought I had committed incest or something. I'm going to ring dad now."

Dario was looking thoroughly confused and Ellie sat down and explained everything.

"Hi dad it's me Sam. Yes thanks Ellie and I are having a great time and I love skiing. Dad I've met a lovely man and I think he is The One. No, no he's nothing like Ralph and no I'm not rushing into anything but he would like to speak to you."

She thrust the phone at Jack who had been smirking since 'the one' bit.

"Hi Frank how are you? Yes it's J ...."

Ellie and Dario left them to their explanations and took Alfie to bed.

Sophie was tucking into her breakfast the following morning when Sam and Jack appeared. Jack winked at Sam.

"Morning sis" said Sam giving her a hug. Sophie looked puzzled and Jack explained about their discovery.

"you are my sister ! " shrieked Sophie leaping up and throwing her arms around Sam, knocking over her juice "I always wanted to meet you, but mum and dad said that you weren't allowed and then after your mum died I was at university." she clapped her hands and started making plans for shopping trips and lunch when they returned.

" I saw you when you were a baby " Sam replied with tears in her eyes. " I wanted to see you again and play with you but I wasn't allowed. I drew some pictures and sent them to you. We will make up for it now."

The three of them went off for their lesson , with their arms around each other and Ellie felt quite emotional.

" It's never a dull moment with you lot is it ? " remarked Poppy " any more hidden boyfriends or brothers, or maybe Phil is your long lost cousin."

Phil grinned " I can't be related to anyone as clumsy as Ellie."

Ellie had knocked her glass of red wine over Phil's white shirt the other evening. He was a perfect gentleman about it , but after that would jokingly refuse to sit anywhere near Ellie. Sam had told them that the staff in Ellie's office would also avoid sitting near her at lunchtime if she was having a salad, after a cherry tomato incident.

" One day I will become elegant and surprise you all " Ellie had retorted laughingly.

CHAPTER SEVENTEEN

Ellie and Alfie met Sam at their usual cafe and Alfie was sitting on the counter being indulged as usual.
"I need to sort things out with work when I get back. I still don't know what I can do here in the winter. It's going to break Alfie's heart when we leave Dario " she sighed " oh hello Alfie I didn't see you there , what have you got now ?"

Alfie was quiet on the walk back to the hotel.
" I think this one is really tired " she said smiling at Alfie. She read him a story and then fell fast asleep in minutes, she had felt really tired today. When she awoke she crept to the bathroom, had a shower and put on some make up. She was just pulling on her jeans in the bedroom when she realised that Alfie wasn't in the pile of bedclothes on his bed. Maybe he had gone to see Sam while she was in the shower. She quickly finished dressing and knocked on Sam's door.
"No I haven't seen him. Now don't panic, let's look in the bedroom. Alfie is a sensible little boy."
"What if he has been abducted , you hear of these things." Ellie's lip was trembling and cold fear had clutched her heart.
" Now is anything missing ?" said Sam
" I, I put his snowsuit and hat and gloves on the radiator and they have gone ! Thinking about it his bed looks the same as when I crept into the shower, which means he left when I was asleep. He has probably been gone for ages. I am really starting to panic now. It's dark outside and cold! "
" Right well you ring Dario and start walking up the road and I will get the others to search the hotel. He might be with Maria and Enzo. Make sure you keep your phone on and try to keep calm. "
Ellie nodded and threw on her boots and jacket. She rang Dario on her way out. He was in a meeting with the other ski instructors. He was horrified but said.
" No si preoccupi cara, don't worry. We will find him. We know all the places in this village, so the other instructors will look. I 'ave an idea."
Ellie walked quickly up the hill looking in all sorts of nooks and crannies. She had a recent photo of Alfie on her phone and showed it to everyone she passed, although it would be hard to recognise him under all his layers. Everyone shook their head. She saw a flash of red snowsuit and grabbed the child. The child turned around and it was a little girl with blond hair.

"Sorry, sorry she said to the surprised parent and showed her the photo. The mother shook her head sadly and pointed to the shops.

" Maybe there "

Ellie couldn't think what would make Alfie leave. Did he want to buy himself a car, or maybe a present for someone ? She rang Sam

" No Sean thought of that. He and Phil have just finished searching the toy car shop. "

"Right I must go I am getting near the ski school meeting place and I can see loads of people searching." a sob caught in her throat " why are they looking in dustbins ?" she started to run and then her phone rang it was Dario.

" I 'ave 'im, 'e was waiting at my 'ouse. come now, 'e is fine, I just getting 'im warm by fire."

"Thank you god, thank you " Ellie had tears streaming down her face. She ran over to one of the searchers and told him that Alfie had been found.

"thank you, thank you for looking and please tell the others and thank them."

The man nodded and smiled

"prego"

Ellie rang Sam and started running to Dario's house. Sam was tearful and said she would tell the others. Ellie stopped outside Dario's house and found a tissue and wiped her face. She didn't want Alfie to see her upset. The door was open and Alfie was sitting on Dario's lap by the fire. He hung his head when he saw her. Sam squatted down in front of him. She put her arms around him.

" Alfie why did you run away we were so worried." and she burst into noisy tears. Alfie hugged her

" I'm really really sorry mummy I didn't mean to make all those people worried. Daddy told me." and he burst into tears and hugged Ellie fiercely.

"Do you know why he did it ? " she asked Dario. Dario nodded

" 'e say that in cafe 'e 'eard you say that 'e would miss me when you leave."

" I fought I would lose my daddy again and I don't ever want to lose him." sobbed Alfie

"Oh Alfie I didn't mean that you wouldn't see your daddy again ! We wouldn't do that to you. You will always have your daddy now. We just need to sort things out when we get home. I can't just leave my job suddenly and we have to talk to gran and grandad. Do you understand ?"

Alfie nodded and they all had a big group hug and shed a few tears.

"promise me an' mummy that you never do that again." said Dario looking sternly at Alfie

" I promise daddy, sorry daddy, sorry mummy."

Dario walked back with them to the hotel. There was a cheer when they walked into the bar and Ellie and Dario were handed much needed drinks.

" I think being father is 'arder than I thought. " sighed Dario " but I not want to change it." smiling at Alfie who was now being hugged by Maria and Enzo. They were giving him a little telling off in Italian and then passed him an enormous banana milk shake.

" If your family are like this there is no hope for him." Ellie said putting her arms around Dario.

" Of course they like this. We are Italian an' we love children." he grinned kissing her cheek "but he will 'ave lots of brothers an' sisters to fight with. Yes ?"

" No I couldn't cope." and she winked at Dario and hopped off the stool.

When she tucked up Alfie in bed that night Ellie said

" Now are you sure you are O.K. now Alfie ? If you have any worries you must always ask me."

" No I'm O.K. " smiled Alfie sleepily "'cept I am a bit worried that you won't be daddy's friend one day, like with Xander."

Ellie stroked Alfie's hair

"well I can't promise that mummy and daddy won't sometimes not be friends, but we will always love you. I hope that I will live with your daddy for ever and ever. You see I love your daddy. I really liked Xander but I didn't love him like I do your daddy. Do you understand."

Alfie nodded

" I am a bit worried too that I can't get all my diggers and cars in my case. Do you think I should leave some with daddy, so I can play with them when I come back? "

" I think that is an excellent idea Alfie. Now night night."

"Night night mummy, love you."

"Ellie come away from the creche and go and ski" said Sam pulling Ellie away from the creche door where she was watching Alfie play.

"I know I am being silly but I don't like letting him out of my sight. I saw Dario ski past and check on him. We are both as bad as each other."

" You both have just had a nasty scare , so it's understandable. Alfie's fine, in fact he seems to be in charge of that little group !"

Alfie was getting the children to queue for the tubes.

" I don't think he realises that Italians don't queue." laughed Ellie. She was beginning to feel less anxious and decided to be a bit daring and try another slope on the other side of the mountain.

It was cold on the chairlift and Ellie started wiggling her fingers. She was a bit nervous when she looked down the new slope but decided to take her own advice and cross it fairly slowly without looking down. She managed to get to the bottom without falling over and felt proud of herself. She stopped off at her usual mountain restaurant and sat outside with a vin brûlée. She shivered it had gradually become more cloudy and had started to snow. she felt quite excited as it had never snowed whilst Ellie had been skiing. People started going down the slope and Ellie thought she had better join them as it was nearly time to collect Alfie. The snow was coming down quite quickly now and looking around there were only a few hardy snowboarders left at the top. Ellie took it really slowly as it was quite disorientating , she nearly missed the turn off for ski school and the creche. She was trying to peer through the snow when she suddenly hit a man who had stopped in the middle of the slope. He had been trying to help the lady he was with who was lying on the ground and Ellie knocked him clean over. He appeared to be German and wasn't very happy.
"Avoid people in front. Take more care!" he shouted.
"I'm terribly sorry. Please let me help you both." She managed to haul them both to their feet and left them to it while she slid down to collect her ski which had flown off. It took her ten minutes to get both skis on as she kept slipping. Her nerves had kicked in and her chest hurt where she had slammed into the man.

Alfie was pleased to see her and really excited about the snow. He kept sticking his tongue out to catch the snowflakes. Dario had asked them to go to his house for lunch as he had made his special minestrone soup.
"No rush as is going to be a wipeout this afternoon, so all lessons cancelled. Listen can you hear that wind ? It not safe to be on slopes this afternoon, but tomorrow will be fine."
Ellie told him about the accident and he shrugged
" accidents happen to everyone. You must stop and check they O.K. an' you did that so don't worry. You sure you O.K. you should have x ray on chest, you might have broken rib."
" No I'm fine . Lets have this soup then."
After lunch Ellie struggled to get out of the chair and Dario could see her wince.
" That's it we take you to medical centre for check. Maybe you have broken rib."

They set off for the medical centre. Luckily it was next to the ski school as snow was drifting across the large car park in the centre of the village. Ellie gave them her insurance details which she kept on her phone. She always travelled with her bank cards in her jacket so was able to pay . She would be able to claim it back later, less the excess. She had an X Ray.

"It is badly bruised" the nurse informed her " you were right to check. If it was broken rib it could pierce lungs or 'eart. You rest now for today and tomorrow take it easy. I give you prescription for painkillers."

"Thanks Dario. I am glad you took me."

" I think after dinner I take Alfie back to my 'ouse to sleep and then tomorrow I take him to creche so you can sleep. Is that O.K.?'

"yes" Ellie smiled " I know he is in good hands and I feel like I could go to sleep now."

Alfie was thrilled that he was going to stay with daddy. He packed his little backpack with penguin, assorted vehicles and sweets.

"Don't you think you will need to pack your pyjamas and clothes for the creche tomorrow? Where did all those sweets come from ? "

"Here " said Alfie opening the drawer in his bedside cabinet. It was full of sweets.

"The nice people in the cafe give them to me and aunty Maria an' uncle Enzo. I don't have room in my tummy for them all."

"well done for not being greedy Alfie. How about on your last day we take some of the sweets and share them with your friends at the creche?"

Alfie thought that was a great idea and started bouncing on the bed. He caught Ellie on the back and when she put her hand up to stop him she found it really painful to lift her arm.

"time for dinner I think and then an early night for me.

CHAPTER EIGHTEEN

The rest of the week went peacefully. Ellie had some bruising and found lifting her arms the most painful. She skied carefully and tried to go on the chairlift with someone else as it hurt to lift the barrier.

Alfie loved the meals that Maria cooked , Ellie didn't know where he put all the food. They all went tobogganing early one evening which was great fun. Alfie sat in front of Ellie or Dario and loved it . "come on mummy we have to try and beat Aunty Sam and Jack. I think daddy is a bit faster than you." He said kindly patting her shoulder when they reached the bottom. Ellie was quite competitive so this resulted in a toboggan race between her and Dario. Of course Dario won but Ellie insisted that her toboggan had been sabotaged.
Every blissful night was spent with Dario.
" I don't want to go home" sighed Ellie
" Nor me " said Sam. I am going to miss everyone, even the grumpy man on the second chairlift. He could see I was having a bit of a problem the other day and didn't slow down the chairlift. If it hadn't been for Jack I would have fallen off. I have even become fond of Poppy and Chloe."
"and me. Do you know they went to that expensive skiwear shop and bought Alfie a lovely ski top. They are really kind."

Alfie had had his last session with Dario earlier and the three of them had done the short blue run back to the village. Alfie had been on the chairlift to the restaurant, but thought it was ' amazing ' to ski off the lift with his skis on. The ski lift man slowed down the lift and Dario held onto one arm. They wended their way slowly down the slope and Alfie only fell over once. At the bottom Dario presented him with a medal, which Alfie then had to show to anyone who was passing.
" I could ski like a pizza an' now I ski like spaghetti, don't I daddy ?"
"You certainly do " replied Dario and then when he saw Ellie looking puzzled " with children we teach snowplough but we call it pizza because of shape and then they start to ski parallel like spaghetti. We don't really have to teach it as kids do it themselves. Like Alfie, did you see he just parallel ski?"
Ellie hadn't she had been too busy concentrating. She just knew that the next time Alfie skied he would be better than her and going faster than her.

Dario had a free slot and they handed Alfie and his medal over to Sam, Jack and Sophie as they were tired from doing the slalom competition and were choosing which hot chocolates to have before handing in their skis and boots.

" Come here Alfie "said Jack "come and choose a hot chocolate. Which one is the best ?"

Alfie took great pleasure in giving them the benefit of his advice.

Dario took Ellie on a long run and gave her some tips to improve her skiing.

"that was the best lesson ever. They always say that a one to one lesson is worth a week of ski school." beamed Ellie putting her feet towards the fire and sipping her mulled wine. They were in the mountain restaurant just before the last run to the village.

" I feel that I really ' get ' skiing now."

" yes you quite good skier now. It because you have best teacher," Dario grinned "come on , we need to check Alfie is OK."

Ellie was about to clip on her skis when a snowball hit her helmet.

"right " she scooped up some snow and tried to shove it down Dario's neck. They ended up having a snow fight much to the bewilderment of the skiers sunbathing outside in deckchairs.

Dario was showing off skiing backwards in front of Ellie. How did people even do that ? Quite a few adults and children shouted ciao to him on the way down, he was obviously a popular teacher.

When they got to the bottom they found that Alfie had discovered how to make a snow angel. He was madly waving his arms. He made Dario lie by him and make a bigger one.

" Only for you Alfie " muttered Dario " people I know will think I crazy."

Ellie lay next to them and made her own snow angel. People were walking past smiling.

Maria said that she and Enzo would babysit Alfie after dinner, so that Ellie and Dario could go and see his friend playing in a bar in the village.

"Is same band " said Dario smiling at Ellie "remember"

" How could I forget " beamed Ellie

It had been agreed that Dario would take them to the airport tomorrow for their late flight and take them to see his family on the way. He only had private lessons booked as it was changeover day and the other instructors were happy to take over the lessons.

Ellie rang Gemma and had a chat with her. She gave her an update "remember that bar we went to to see the band and we arrived early ?"

"oh yes the bombardino bar" replied Gemma " I wish I was there with you now."

"Well Dario and I are going tonight "

" It sounds to me that we might be losing you from work. Should I warn Mark ?"

" I think maybe, but we are still trying to sort out the logistics."

"Well make sure you do everything you can to stay with Dario. I blame myself, I should have ignored you and contacted Hotel Girasole or the ski school.when you found that you were pregnant "

"It's not your fault I was so stubborn " sighed Ellie " At least thanks to Sam it's all turned out well. Did I tell you about Sam ? " and she proceeded to give her an update on Sam's lovelife.

" It all sounds very romantic. If you decide to live in Italy, Mark and I will come and visit you and maybe have a skiing holiday before we start a family."

"Sounds like a plan. See you next week."

Ellie was getting ready for dinner when she received a message from Sean. He and Phil had decided to go a bit further afield on their last day. They had got lost and missed the last chairlift back on the last leg. Ellie rang Dario.

" No worries I will pick them up in my car."

Everyone had just sat down to dinner and they all clapped when the wanderers returned . Maria insisted that Dario stay to dinner. Alfie was in high spirits during dinner and thrilled that his daddy was having dinner with them. He insisted on sitting next to Dario and Ellie's heart melted looking at the two of them together. Two peas in a pod. They started chatting to each other in Italian.

"That's so lovely that he can speak Italian and he is only three." marvelled Sophie.

Alfie was still wearing his medal. He had flipped it to the back so that it wouldn't get in his soup.

" Hey Alfie I have won a medal too" Sophie said " I am collecting it later , we can wear our medals together tomorrow."

" Yes " Alfie nodded solemnly " Did my daddy give you your medal ? "

" No Alfie ,it was my ski instructor, yours is a special medal isn't it."

" yes and it's extra special 'cos I'm only three you know and I can ski spaghetti now. Can you /"
Sophie had to admit that she couldn't.

" Me and daddy will teach you." he said patting her hand kindly

They all sat around the fire afterwards. Sean and Phil both looked a bit sunburnt after their experience.

" we won't need disco lights we can dance around you two." teased Ellie

" shut up and bring us a drink " replied Phil waving money at Ellie " We could have been stuck in the middle of nowhere if it hadn't been for your gorgeous man. I am shattered, we must have covered a few miles today. Get him a drink too and make it a double." " and yourself " he added with a wink and blew her a kiss.

Alfie waved them off happily and disappeared into the back room with Enzo to carry on with something they were making.They walked up to the presentation together. Dario was looking very handsome as he and the other instructors changed into blazers for the presentation. Sophie had won the slalom race for her group and insisted on wearing her medal to the bar after. They all cheered Sophie when she stood on the podium. Then they walked across to the bar to see the band.

She had had fun chatting to different men but she said she was too young to get serious yet. She had plans to go to Australia next year. Jack had had a gap year and she wanted to do the same. "but before that you and I are going to have some girlie fun." she said linking arms with Sam. Sam looked so happy that Ellie went and hugged them both and shed a tear. If she managed to go and live in Italy then her best friend would not be alone.

They were all in great spirits and a DJ was playing music. Ellie managed to get Dario to dance. He was quite a good dancer, just a bit shy. Then some of the Italians did a zumba type line dance to some Latin music. Ellie and Sophie joined in, everyone seemed to know exactly what they were doing and then they did another. It was really good although Ellie and Sophie didn't have a clue what they were doing.

Some of the ski instructors had come to the bar after the presentation. Chloe and Poppy were flirting as usual, but kept asking if they had seen Antonio. One of the instructors came over to Dario and they had a long conversation, with much waving of arms. Dario looked surprised and then he and the instructor burst out laughing. Dario came back chuckling.

"What's the matter ?" Ellie asked. Dario smiled

"I should not smile, but you know Antonio, he been taking those girls on private lesson"

"yes" replied Ellie and leaves them in the bar to 'rest ' while he prays to Jesus. "

Dario grinned " well he no pray to Jesus, he meet his friend Jesus over the Swiss border and give him stolen jewellery. He was arrested this afternoon . The police say they been watching him for long time, as he is accused in Switzerland before but no proof. "

"no!" exclaimed Ellie "who is going to tell the girls ?"

The 'girls ' were quite indignant .

"I wondered why he always had that big rucksack" said Chloe " he said it was emergency supplies . What a nob."

" He was nice though" said Poppy

"yea he was " said Chloe with a dreamy smile on her face " a bit like James Bond really. Just think we could have been arrested while we were skiing with a famous jewel thief. Wait until we tell our friends at home" I need to add some photos of us with him on Instagram as he will probably be in the news and she shimmied across the dance floor, followed by Poppy flicking her hair back.

Dario and Ellie raised their eyebrows at each other . They listened to the band's first set, had one last dance and decided to go back to Alfie.

They spent the night in the hotel together and Ellie couldn't help but remember the last time they had done this, the night before she flew home. What was going to happen to her and Alfie now ?

"I can sleep when I get home." she thought as she lay gazing at Dario and worrying about the future. The moon was shining through the curtains and lighting up Dario's face. Ellie lay watching him for ages before she fell asleep and when she awoke Dario was watching her.

"Stop it."

" You do it to me. Are you excited meeting my family ? I can't wait to show them you and Alfie.I have been awake or an hour "

Ellie nodded, she had a headache and hadn't slept well.

CHAPTER NINETEEN

Ellie was a bundle of nerves , she hadn't slept well as it had taken her ages to drop off and then she had had a nightmare about Dario's nonna hitting her with a broom. Dario had gone back to his house to collect some things for his parents. Alfie was bounding around jumping on the bed while she tried to pack.

"stop it Alfie, keep still for a minute" she snapped. Alfie's bottom lip wobbled and his eyes filled with tears

"but I am excited cus I'm meeting another gran and grandad today and a big gran"

"I am sorry Alfie " said Ellie giving him a hug and kiss "I am just a bit worried because I have never met daddy's family before and it's great gran , not big gran !"

"don't worry mummy, they will be nice like daddy and I will hold your hand."

Ellie hugged him again, she didn't want to leave Dario, but she would miss her family and what would happen if she came to live here, she felt scared. She couldn't be a ski instructor and much as she had loved her skiing week she didn't think she wanted to live in the village all winter. There were no estate agents in Barganago. She had discussed it with Sam and had been pondering it all night, because she couldn't bear to lose Dario now that she had found him again. She couldn't see Dario settling in the Cotswolds, what would he do ! Ellie finished packing and started pacing up and down, then Sam knocked on the door and helped carry the luggage downstairs.

Everyone hugged Ellie, Alfie and Dario when they left after breakfast. The coach was not picking up the others until after lunch and they would see Sam, Jack and Sophie at the airport. The others were catching a different flight. Ellie had exchanged phone numbers with Sean and Phil and they had promised to keep her updated regarding the adoption."I can give you good references" Ellie laughed. Poppy and Chloe gave Ellie a lovely scarf to wear meeting the in laws. They were so kind. They were also thrilled that they now had lots more instagram followers as 'James Bond's girls".

Ellie hugged Sam

" thank you for the best holiday ever "

"I think it's my best holiday ever and I have come back with extra luggage ." said Sam smiling at Jack who blew her a kiss.

Maria and Enzo waved them off in Dario's car.

"see you soon" said Maria " now you make sure you come back and see your aunty Maria and uncle Enzo " and she pinched Alfie's cheeks and kissed him. Alfie ran back and gave them another hug. They would miss Alfie , their daughter was studying hard at school and Ellie hadn't seen much of her, except when she helped out as waitress in the evening. Their son was grown up so maybe they would be grandparents soon. Alfie appeared to be clutching several more vehicles and she could see what looked like a crane sticking out of his pocket. He blew kisses to them all the way down the road.

" I am going to 'ave trouble with this one" said Dario grinning at Ellie. then he frowned " Are you O.K. you very quiet ."

" I am really scared that your family will be cross with me for keeping Alfie from them, they didn't get to see him when he was a baby."

" Shush is not going to happen, they just pleased to meet you both now. They shout at me a little for letting you go. Anyway we can make more beautiful babies. You like a little brother or sister Alfie yes ?"

Ellie gulped .

They drove for forty five minutes while Alfie chattered to Dario . The mountainous area gave way to hills and beautiful villages with terracotta roofs. It was Ellie's idea of heaven. Oh to live somewhere like this. Ellie and her parents used to dream about buying a holiday home on the edge of a beautiful old village. They used to talk about owning a house on the edge of a village and then walking into the village to buy their bread and have a morning coffee and then going back in the evening for a meal. They drove through a picture postcard village and she caught a glimpse of a wonderful piazza , which was edged by bars. Ellie could imagine how it would look in the summer, full of people eating, drinking and chatting. The weather would be wonderful too.

Dario pulled up outside a large farmhouse just outside the village. He held a key out to Alfie
" Now Alfie press this button and say ' open sesame ' " Alfie pressed the key and shouted
" Open sesame" at the top of his voice. He looked amazed when the gates slowly opened " wow I did that didn't I daddy ?" He bounded out of the car with Dario while Ellie hung back. Dario came back and put his arm around her shoulders.
"come on we are not so bad."

She smiled at him and nervously tidied her hair. The door was opened by a cheery lady wearing an apron.

" Dario caro " and then she looked at Alfie and enveloped him in a big hug.

" I am your nonna " she said with tears running down her face and then she turned to Ellie and hugged her "welcome welcome."

They followed her into a large kitchen and there were Dario's father and grandmother. There were more hugs and tears .

"here we go again more crying" sighed Alfie rolling his eyes as Dario's nonna released him from the biggest hug ever.

Dario's parents laughed, but his grandmother could not speak English. Ellie knelt down by Alfie and whispered "Daddy's grandma can't speak English so can you speak to them in Italian please. "certo " replied Alfie and proceeded to chatter away to them in Italian which caused more tears, although nonna enquired why her great grandson spoke like a Roman !

Dario's grandmother beckoned Ellie over "Grazie for leetle Alfreddo" she said giving Ellie a smacking kiss." then in Italian she said "Dario he should not have let you go but was a hard time for us."

" yes I am so sorry I didn't know.' stuttered Ellie in Italian.

" no matter now. We have a beautiful boy and 'is mama. " said Dario's mum giving Ellie another hug.

The house was an old farmhouse with wooden beams and terracotta floors. The walls were painted cream and there was a beautiful kitchen that looked old but was obviously quite new. There was a large covered terrace at the rear, with wonderful views backed by mountains. Ellie's mom and dad would be in raptures over this house.

They all sat down to lunch . They chattered away and although Ellie's Italian had improved Dario had to stop to translate. He also asked them to speak more slowly, which they did and then they would get excited and forget. Food kept appearing on the table and finally Dario's nonna produced a large bowl and placed it in front of Ellie with a smile.

"Tiramisu " cried Alfie " that's our favourite isn't it mummy ?" He then went quiet while he wolfed down a huge bowlful.

"you are right it is ten " he mumbled between mouthfuls. They explained to nonna and she clapped her hands and laughed and then gave them both more. At this rate they would have to watch they weren't sick on the plane. The meal had been wonderful but the family kept plying them with food.
" No thank you I have no more room " said Ellie waving away the cheese. They asked quite a few questions which Dario helped her translate. Alfie however didn't seem to have a problem and often answered the questions before Dario had finished translating. He proudly showed them his medal and they clapped him and got him to pose with it while they took his photo. Then they took photos of Ellie, Dario and Alfie.
" I am going to have big photo of you here." said nonna and pointed to the cabinet at the side. She picked up a framed photo of a man who looked very much like Dario.
" This is my Alfreddo " she said in Italian. Ellie told her that he looked very handsome and she was sorry that she had never met him. Dario's nonna nodded and hugged her.

" I think I have to make you a swimming pool hey ? " said Dario's dad
" really nonno " exclaimed Alfie his eyes wide in wonder then carried on in Italian " I can swim a bit but need my arm bands .Can you swim " he asked each of his grandparents and great grandmother. Her shoulders shook with laughter as she shook her head. Alfie knelt down beside her and patted her hand.
" Never mind I will teach you when I am a bit bigger" . She nodded and replied that she could ski and she picked up a photo of his great grandparents dressed in old fashioned skiing gear. This really impressed Alfie. He then dragged his grandfather outside and spent the next half hour leading him to different places that he thought would be good for a pool. Ellie could hear him saying
" Nonno I think you would really like it if you had a slide on your pool. You and nonna could slide down it together."

Dario's parents had been whispering with Dario and then Dario's dad said
" Dario show Ellee the surprise. She has to go to airport soon."
"come Alfie" said Dario leading them both out of the house. They crossed the olive grove and walked along a path beside the vineyard until they came to a cluster of barns. They were in good repair but didn't look as if they were used any longer. The view from the rear of the barns was magnificent. It swept across vineyards and olive trees and was backed by pale purple mountains. This place was heaven.

" I can't believe how beautiful this place is. I don't think I have ever seen a better view." breathed Ellie.

" Yes it is very beautiful but my father he build new barns near the house for the machines and grapes and we don't have animals here now. So is not needed. "

He then dropped to one knee

"Ellee, Ellee I love you and I love Alfie, will you marry me ? My family they say we can have these barns and use the beeg one for us and make the others 'oliday 'omes. What you think?' he looked at Ellie anxiously " I know I ask a lot for you to leave your home. This can be our job as we can make enough money from renting three barns to live good life and maybe the swimming pool should be here for Alfie and the visitors"

"but what about skiing you love it . I can't ask you to stop skiing."

"I love you more and I have spoken to ski school. They are happy for me to work at weekends and then five weeks a year at busiest times . You could go back to England with Alfie then. You could go back when you want.You could come to nonno"s house at weekends and ski, Alfie you would like that eh ?" Also we can make one of the barns into house for your mama and papa and they can come when they like. We can make big barn into beautiful house for us an' our children. We can have best life here."

Ellie gave a choked reply "Yes please yes yes yes " and she flung herself into Dario's arms. Alfie wriggled his way in-between them and looked at Ellie.

"Oh mummy said Alfie "now you are crying too.

THE END

Printed in Great Britain
by Amazon